THIS BOOK BELONGS TO

I0621365

An A-Girl Studio book
published 2017 in the USA.

For additional information, please contact:
A-Girl Studio
P.O. Box 213, Burbank, CA 91503 U.S.A.
www.a-girlstudio.com

ISBN: 978-1-936622-11-5

First paperback edition, 2017

BODY CHASE

OR

THE FALL

OF

FAIRER THAN

Volume 3

By
Elizabeth Watasin

CHAPTER ONE

Across the mist-covered seas, on the shrouded edges of the known and mundane, lay the Twilight World. There, forgotten kingdoms rose and fell, and modest little modern towns dotted the ancient forest interior, home to monsters and magical people. In the town of Little Salem, a good teen witch named Bunny Baker lived. A daughter of a seventh daughter, she happened to be in love with a vampire named Dean, while a dark faerie happened to be in love with Bunny.

Fairer Than the Fairest of All Faeries, notorious seducer and homewrecker, sought to win Bunny twice and lost, nearly killing Dean in the process. Though Dean was Bunny's chosen, rejection did not sit well with a dark faerie that was also part human and part dragon.

Fairer Than stood by the Baker cottage's low garden wall under cover of night and exhaled. Smoke left her nostrils, but she smoked no cigarette or pipe.

Fairer Than was hard put to define her feelings for Bunny as true "love." Desire, yes, and a deep fondness and appreciation, assuredly. She wanted her. But being half faerie, she was perhaps incapable of true love. Her heart, in the tradition of her dragon brethren, was hidden in a goose egg, in a sealed chest, under a great stone, beneath a man-eating maelstrom. Perhaps Fairer Than could not love, but her infatuation remained rather than waned, and became a persistent smoldering in her thoughts and upon her senses.

Thus, Fairer Than found that the heart-shadow occupying the heart-shaped space within her breast was prone to discontent and—to her horror—foolish sighing, especially when she stood within view of Bunny Baker's cottage window. There, Fairer Than might watch Bunny move about in her bedroom.

She knew she was behaving, in the local vernacular, "like a creep," but whatever had enslaved her heart-shadow inspired her to such foolish demonstrations.

"Alas," she said by the low stonewall.

Then Bunny's aunties would leap out of hiding and douse her with the water hose.

Introducing: Honey

Bunny, as a daughter of a seventh daughter, had many aunties, and though the three aunties she lived with never bore children, her other three had. Bunny's cousins all happened to be girls, all were witches, and all of them, like Bunny, had been raised on cream, eggs, and butter, and therefore were very pretty.

One day, one such cream-and-butter cousin walked up a path of the Enchanting Forest in search of Bunny's cottage. Honey-haired and generous of breast, thighs, and hips, this elder cousin of Bunny was named Honey. Honey Baker did not have a great sense of direction. If she had a basket of goodies for grandmother she would never make it to grandmother's house—not that she would ever intentionally visit that frightening crone, anyway. Accidentally visit her, perhaps, but not with firm purpose in heart and hand.

"If only I hadn't said I needed to see Bunny." Honey blew at the wave of hair that fell over one eye. "I'd be there already!"

She set her pointed, black hat determinedly on her head and followed the path again. She had nearly come by broom, but even with landmarks as her guide, she could still lose her way within a hundred feet of Bunny's cottage. The family had said that getting lost was her gift. She would then discover things—important things—aside from her original destination. She would stumble upon hidden treasure, rescue someone in distress, or plain meddle in some important affair of dire consequence. Princes and princesses, evil or otherwise, in several realms, had reason to curse her or court her for foiling or aiding in their plans. Such luck on her part gave the family an excuse to never send her on errands, nor was she expected to keep appointments or arrive on time for engagements.

But that day she had an urgent purpose.

She'd started her morning taking the wash out to hang, yet somehow—after pursuing an errant clothes peg out the garden gate—ended up down by the bubbling Lava River and entering a sulphuric-smelling grotto. There, a ritual was in progress.

Virgin priestesses in their diaphanous veils were partaking of the odious vapors. A party of dignitaries awaited what they might say. Honey set her basket of wash down, took a seat, and watched the ritual of dropping henbane into gaseous hollows, a sight she'd never had the pleasure of witnessing before. The waiting, wizened dignitaries, in officious uniforms, robes, and hats—some in embroidered Chinese silks with tall hats—appeared to be vampires; of that she was certain for some did not walk but hopped.

Is that a seneschal? Honey peered at one little man in a very tall hat whose long, belted gown and finger rings marked him as a possible steward. In her line of work, she'd never met a steward who wasn't evil or at least mildly corrupt. Which was a sad thing to assume, but Honey's talent for flukes tended to lead her to people needing defeating, and not often enough to content and happy people.

The chosen oracle fell into trance and spoke in a strange and distant voice:

> *They can, so they will*
> *break Balance, feed on Misery*
> *with the men who rise, again and again*
> *led by a female prince of their kind*
> *her true love of white gold, bread, and seven to stop her.*

The oracle then ceased speaking and collapsed into the arms of her companions.

The vampires shook hands with each other, seemingly pleased. Their attendees loaded each of their decrepit masters and mistresses into horse-drawn carriages or lacquered *jiaos* and bore them swiftly away. Honey's heart pounded as she wrote down the prophesy in her pocket diary, attached to her pencil skirt's patent leather and silver buckled black belt via a round steel pin and its retractable chain. She let her diary go—the thin chain retracting—picked up her wash, and hurried down to the swooning oracle.

"You mentioned bread," Honey said as the priestesses revived their sister. The woman's glassy gaze remained lost in viewing unseen realms.

"A baker," she uttered.

"Yes, that's me. But now I understand. The word *seven* is the key." Honey nodded determinedly as the oracle closed her eyes. "Thanks." Honey hefted her wash and climbed out of the grotto.

Honey had heard a few riddles as well as prophesies in her time, whether from dark faeries cursing queens or little men entrapping young women. But the oracle's words had been clear. *White gold* could describe three of Honey's cousins by their hair color; *seven* could only describe one.

Her platinum-haired cousin, Bunny, was the daughter of the seventh Baker daughter.

And the identity of the female prince was easy.

Bunny's girlfriend, Dean, was destined to become Golden Bloody Overlord of the One Thousand Vampire Horde.

❧

When a purpose came Honey's way, her ability to get directly somewhere became without obstacle. No longer was she Honey, the Flukey Witch, but Honey, Witch with a Mission. Thus, after hanging up the wash and her apron and grabbing a defensive spell left on the entryway console by her older sister, Sugar, she proceeded to Bunny's.

Silverdale, the valley town in which Honey lived, was surrounded by one dormant volcano and imposing mountains. The mountain pass to Bunny's hometown in the Enchanting Forest could easily be traversed by motor vehicle. But unlike Sugar, Honey did not know how to drive, much less something with hellfire injection, and she did not like to travel by broomstick. She used the witch's shortcut, a maze maintained at the town's public garden.

Honey concentrated on getting to Bunny's cottage and walked the maze with a *Welcome*! tourist postcard of Little Salem held before her. When she emerged, she stood before a *This Way to Little Salem* sign erected in the woods, just like in her postcard.

Half an hour later, she seemed no nearer to town, despite hearing its clock tower chime the hour. Her discoveries for the day were perhaps not done. She wasn't in the mood for another revelation. She needed to pee.

Honey entered a great clearing where rowdy laughter sounded from an old timber lodge. Gleaming motorcycles sat parked. The painted sign read: *The Dog & Whistle*. Honey tiptoed past a snoring old lady in a babushka, her wooden walking stick laid across her broad lap as she napped on a bench. The double-paned glass revealed nothing, but the stench of ale was strong. Honey touched the little pouch hanging from her belt: Sugar's ready-made spell.

She set her chin, pulled open the heavy door to a raucous din, and entered. Pushing through the creatures and people, she headed for the clearly marked ladies' room.

When Honey eventually emerged, pencil skirt smoothed out, lipstick touched up, hair brushed, and hat straightened, she took in the tavern crowd. It was barely midday, but the place was already packed with demon bikers in leather gear, devil salesmen in wrinkled suits hunching at the bar top, and crones in babushkas and flower-embroidered skirts circling the pool table with their cues. Honey couldn't identify the sort of Other-being the powerful fellow with great antlers might be—a possible stag spirit or even a minor deity—but she assumed the human-looking folk were supernatural, at least in that part of the Twilight World.

Her adventures in getting lost sometimes took her to villages where only humans existed, caught in space/time like the magical beings. Ordinary folk were equally likely to either accept Honey's witchyness or not (especially where evil, sorceress queens existed). Escaping executions and angry mobs was not easy. Honey was always grateful to be back where everyone was as different as she was.

Sometimes demigods walked among Other-beings and ordinary folk, radiating a power that attracted all creatures like bees to flowers, and inspired the foolhardy into flinging challenge. It was a thrill knowing such beings dallied in their midst.

Oddly, Honey was feeling the radiating presence of a significant being right then; one that made her think of fire, flowers, and bowers.

She looked at the man with antlers. He noticed and gave

her a suave look. She ignored him and turned for a table in a carved booth.

A faerie sat with tumbling red hair dotted with tiny, white flowers. Her long and voluptuous body was clad in a deep green kirtle with a brief bodice dangling loose laces. On one bicep she wore a gold armlet. Honey didn't need to look under the table to know the woman's feet were bare. She had heavy-lidded green eyes and pouty lips and Honey thought her a sweet-smelling fire she wouldn't mind sitting close to and breathing in.

The faerie had just concluded a very bawdy tale for her table companions and was laughing uproariously for one of her highly mannered kin. Several tankards sat empty, and young women in tight sweaters and pencil skirts flanked her: a fox girl of red with white markings on her face, and a cat girl of jet-black with golden eyes. Both were human-looking in body and features. A devil girl sat on the table and showed off her silk stockings, while a ghost girl wearing rhinestone frames hovered next to the fox girl, enjoying her beer.

Honey's smile at the bawdy tale faded when she realized who the redhead was: the part human, part *dragon* faerie known as Fairer Than, who'd tried to win Bunny on Sweetheart's Day by nearly killing Dean.

Really! Indignant, Honey watched as Fairer Than laughed again at something the devil girl said. It appeared that Bunny was the least on the carousing faerie's mind.

"Wench!" Fairer Than suddenly called to Honey. "You must be new. Give me that flagon on the table's edge, will you?" She waved to the full pitcher in question, though the smirking devil girl sat right next to it.

Honey walked up, rested her hands on the table, and

leaned over the flagon.

"I'd heard you were this—big *rogue*, but to see it for myself!" she exclaimed. "If I were Bunny and you'd nearly killed my love just to have me, I'd tell you a thing or two."

"You are denying me my ale, that's punishment enough. Who are you?" Fairer Than peered.

"I'm Honey Baker." Honey straightened. "Bunny's cousin. Here on an important mission. And after what I'd heard from that oracle, I'd honestly thought, well, maybe you should have killed Dean. It would have made Bunny sad, but things would be simpler. Especially when all we witches weren't too keen on her being with a vampire, anyway. But now that I've seen you, I'm reminded that you're no better."

"What *are* you talking about?" Fairer Than frowned.

Honey looked at her sternly. "You've been nothing but the talk of the witch folk, the way you continue to stalk Bunny and make her poor aunties chase you away."

"Little old ladies need their exercise." Fairer Than raised a tankard to her lips and then upturned it, empty. "And as for this 'stalking'—ha! Why should Bunny matter to me? I'm no more her concern than she is mine."

"That's right. Why should she care if you're getting soused and—and cavorting? At least from what I know, Dean wouldn't act like you."

"Oh yes." Fairer Than's lip curled. "The *vampire*."

"You still want to cause trouble?" Honey raised a brow.

"Trouble is what I cause solely for myself." Fairer Than sat back and placed arms around the fox girl and cat girl, who both snuggled close. "Bunny is not the only girl in town. Would you like to join us?"

Honey gasped.

"I jest. Seducing you would be like seducing Bunny's sibling. A poorly conceived plan I had the foolishness to try once in Verona, which I'll never try again."

"I'm not her sister! And I still wouldn't put it past you to make a pass, despite what you say, you dragon-thing!"

But Fairer Than's heavy-lidded gaze had already slid away, apparently focused on drunken thoughts. Honey turned around in a huff.

And therefore did not see when Fairer Than suddenly reached for the flagon of ale behind Honey. The devil girl grabbed Fairer Than's hand and smacked it against Honey's backside.

Honey turned back as the girls laughed. Fairer Than stared stupidly.

"Why, you!" Honey cried.

"But—" Fairer Than said.

Honey took the pouch from her belt and flung the contents in Fairer Than's face.

The other girls jumped back and the ghost girl turned invisible. Powdered sugar glittered as Fairer Than inhaled, then coughed mightily. It dusted Fairer Than's hair and shoulders. The particles faded to weak twinkles and disappeared.

Honey turned the pouch over to reveal Sugar's writing.

"*By this cast, shall you switch!*" Honey read quickly. "*To your complement, become polar opposites! Banish, vanish, relive!*"

She waited. Fairer Than continued to cough and wipe at her eyes. The girls looked from her to Honey.

Oh. Isn't it harder to make spells stick to dragons?

Fairer Than rose. A golden girdle of ancient medallions and large, sharp teeth hung around her hips.

"Why," she said, her eyes tearing, "did you fling sugar at me?"

"I'm not sure. Bye!" Honey hurried for the door.

Once the tavern door slammed shut behind her, Honey ran for the path she'd abandoned. She didn't think Fairer Than would harm her, but Honey wasn't certain if staying longer in the dark faerie's company was wise either. The legendary allure of those of dragon's blood had become evident, even to one like Honey, who hadn't as strong an attraction for girls as Bunny did.

She heard Little Salem's clock tower chime again and resolved to forget having met such an infuriating and seductive creature. She headed in the chime's direction.

CHAPTER TWO
The Vampire Prince

In a forest bower made of woven branches and softened with rushes and fragrant flowers, Fairer Than entertained the cat girl from the tavern.

Inky, the cat girl, and her friends, the devil girl, fox girl, and ghost girl, presumably came into the tavern to play pool but the Russian crones dominated the table. Dressed and made up like young women hoping for a good time whilst on a day off from work—which in Little Salem could be a job as shop girl, beautician, telephone operator, or an acolyte of Bastet's temple—they ignored the devil salesmen who perked up on their barstools and headed for Fairer Than's table. They smelled of perfume and glittered with drop earrings, charm bracelets, and chain necklaces with single silver initials, resting on their tight sweater fronts.

"Why aren't you girls at the moving pictures?" Fairer Than asked in good humor. Like Bunny, they seemed too respectable for the seedy environs of a tavern, which was exactly why Fairer Than had chosen the place.

"We heard there was a movie star, right here," the devil girl answered. She touched Fairer Than's shoulder, than slid on to the table to sit. "I'm Dina. This is Velma, Penny, and Inky," she introduced, pointing to the fox girl, ghost girl, and the cat girl. "Can we have your autograph?"

Fairer Than denied being a celluloid actress and the girls feigned surprise, declaring Fairer Than had to be Jane Russell, except with red hair. Fairer Than didn't know who "Jane Rustle" was but somehow she'd become the ladies' chosen entertainment and welcomed the company. She invited them to join her, ordered drinks, and regaled her new companions with stories.

Inky remained quiet through all the laughter and banter, refused drinks, and sat close enough to press against Fairer Than's side, staring at her with half-closed, golden eyes. Fairer Than wondered if Inky's animal form was a little black cat or a black panther, because if the former, she might prefer a milk.

She became aware of something more when Inky pressed closer; Inky smelled of the l'eau de toilette Bunny favored. Damascene roses and jasmine.

"I'm Bunny's cat," Inky whispered.

Fairer Than's arm was around Inky's waist before she thought to ask permission. She held a little part of Bunny, even if that part was her cat.

After the exasperating encounter with Bunny's cousin (who, besides being plumper and with differently colored hair, had looked so much like Bunny that Fairer Than was unsettled) Inky began to purr. Her friends moved away and found other distractions.

Fairer Than's boisterous pretense fled, and she pushed her tankard away.

"My problems are my own," she said, "and I hate a maudlin drunk as much as anyone."

Inky slowly blinked, her eyes large and golden.

"Oh, just ask," she said, her tone mild.

"Do you know why she is with that lout?" Fairer Than demanded.

Inky purred, her lids half-closed. Cats and foxes knew the reasons for things. But true to their mysterious natures, they never answered what might seem self-evident (at least to them) or was terribly boring. Right then, Inky might not be dwelling on Fairer Than's question, but on cream or mice.

"Do you know why you want to be Bunny's lout?" Inky then asked.

"I only wanted to seduce the girl. Now...she occupies my heart's shadow. If she must have a lout, I can make a better one than the vampire," Fairer Than asserted, glum.

Inky purred more.

Fairer Than touched Inky's hand, found acceptance, and left the tavern with her. After a pleasant walk in which she caused catnip to sprout, she picked a sprig for Inky. Fairer Than invited the cat girl into her bower. Inky lost no time falling into her arms.

"Fairer Than!" a tiny voice called from her bower's entrance.

Fairer Than pulled her mouth from Inky's and sat up, her companion in her lap. A green grasshopper dressed in a blue frock coat and carrying a fiddle, hopped into her bower.

"Ahem!" He puffed, self-important. "I bring you a summons from our Queen, who, no doubt displeased by your continued consorting with witches—"

"I have been consorting with no witches, much to mine own displeasure," Fairer Than said.

The grasshopper harrumphed. "A witch who nearly set the forest *on fire* on Sweetheart's Night, Fairer Than—"

"As might happen due to a woman's justifiable wrath, as Titania well knows. But good and strong women know to rein such power, and that was what Bunny Baker did. Do not dwell on that which never happened," Fairer Than chastised, "or you'll be telling our Queen lies. Begone."

She blew a puff of air at the grasshopper, sending him tumbling from her bower.

"Ah! *Fairer Than!*" he cried from afar, but said nothing more.

"Where were we?" Fairer Than smiled at Inky.

Inky pushed Fairer Than to the bower's floor.

Like all cat people, Inky was very curious, and Fairer Than lay back, indulgent, letting her discover all she needed to know. But Fairer Than politely requested that Inky remain human looking, because Fairer Than was not the sort of woman who could kiss animals with passion, like swans, toads, or horses.

And when Fairer Than's mind wandered, she forced it back to the girl present in her bower. Such commingling was meant to solve a problem. Women's bodies, voices, and gazes made her forget. Not since leaving her first and last wife (whom she'd married whilst in the form of a man) for that foolish lark called a Crusade had she missed someone so terribly.

Alas.

"Oh, don't be like that," Inky said.

Fairer Than looked at her, surprised.

"Now why are you with me?" Inky asked, her large

pupils rimmed with gold.

"You are beautiful," Fairer Than said, and Inky smiled, her finger tracing Fairer Than's lip.

"When you don't need girls like me," Inky said softly, "then things might get clearer."

Fairer Than was oddly comforted by Inky's words, despite not understanding them (and as was usual with cats, they said little that was immediately helpful). Inky kissed Fairer Than again.

"And remember," Inky suddenly said, "If I don't get to shift to cat form, you don't get to change, too. I heard you dragon types can get me pregnant."

"In my woman's form, I can't."

Inky moved Fairer Than's hands lower.

Fairer Than was about to help Inky with her skirt, when—

A shuddering—

Pulled—

Hard enough to snatch her to somewhere. She released Inky and gripped the ground.

"What's happening?" Alarmed, Inky grabbed Fairer Than's face.

Before Fairer Than could say, she was gone.

Dean strutted down a Little Salem street, doo-wop playing in her head.

Haunt High's students rushed by in hot rods and on flying broomsticks for lunch break. Dean pulled out her comb from a back pocket and ran it through her slicked duck-tailed hair. Comb back in pocket she turned up her black leather jacket's collar. She rolled the toothpick in her mouth, tucked it against a fang, and grinned.

If I could take you to paradise way above,
ah langa dinga ding-dong

She was a biker without a motorcycle thanks to her buddy Danny running it over, but that day she didn't mind not roaring down the street, leaving flames in her wake. Since surviving her race in Hell, small moments had become worth savoring. Right then she was taking in Little Salem's sights like Bunny would, walking from school everyday. For once, Dean wasn't sitting in a detention room for fighting and could be with her girl.

"Orange," she said, spying the biggest one displayed in a crate outside a green grocer. She grabbed the bright fruit and flipped the green man a coin.

Next-door was a spice vendor's storefront, full of fragrant display cases with piles of colorful ground spices. Metal scoops and stiff paper with written prices were sunk into the piles. Dean walked in and pointed at the whole cloves in the box between the cinnamon sticks and star anise.

"A handful of that, right there," she said. The vendor put the requested amount into a white paper bag, folded it closed, and handed it to Dean. Dean emerged from the shop, smirking and holding her white bag and orange.

Sha-lang a lang a whoa-oh

She approached the beauty shop, where two beauticians in sunglasses dawdled out front. One had a skull face with a crack in the forehead, while the other was a devil girl with petite horns and a big flower pinned in her hair. Both wore tight skirts beneath their smocks.

"Hey Dean," the skull girl said.

"Hey Dean," the devil girl said.

"'Ey," Dean greeted with a grin and strutted by.

But when she neared Shivers, the soda shop, her strut slowed. Inside, students chatted at the tables, eating their Blood Burgers and Ghost Fries. Madeline, the Gorgon girl, sat with her friends in a window booth. They seemed to be having a good time, except Maddy was staring out the window, her gaze unseeing. Even the snakeheads of her gently waving hair looked pensive.

Dean knew that Maddy and her mummy boyfriend, Scott, had been fighting. He would have been sitting with Maddy right then. With all that happened on Sweetheart's Day—the hell race, the death match with Fairer Than— Dean hadn't time to find out if Maddy and Scott had broken up for good.

Maddy's friends looked Dean's way, and then put their heads together to whisper. Dean mustered a smile, threw open the door, and walked in to the beat of the jukebox. Anxiety gripped when she saw that the first stools at the countertop were empty.

Then she spotted Bunny. Seated at the end, her platinum hair waving over one eye, Bunny had her black, pointed hat set aside. She wore a short-sleeved blouse and mid-length, black pencil skirt, one foot nearly slipping out of a black flat as she toed the counter's bar rest. She was sucking on the straw of her milkshake, a specially made drink Dean knew would have two raw eggs whipped into it. When Dean neared, Bunny's hazel eyes lit.

"Dean," Bunny said warmly, and the sound of her voice made Dean feel ten times taller.

"Hey," Dean said, giving her a kiss. She handed Bunny the fruit and paper bag.

"Oh, Dean! An orange—and cloves? Did you want me

to make a pomander?" Bunny teased. She opened the bag to peek, possibly guessing the contents from the fragrance.

"A what?" Dean said. "Is that good luck? Because that's what the orange is for, and the cloves are just something I know you always use. In baking and stuff."

Bunny looked at her expectantly, smiling.

"Not that I'm telling you to go bake, or something," Dean said quickly. "I just mean, maybe for spells, or other good things—you like them, right?"

Bunny laughed. "Thank you."

She reached for Dean's face and Dean gladly bent to kiss her again.

"An orange for 'Good luck,' or do ya mean 'good will'?" she heard a snide voice ask from beside Bunny.

The voice belonged to the little red demon, Pippita, seated on a stool next to Bunny. Her short and stout stature belied the kind of damage the horned schemer could work. Right then, her pointy tail was straight up from her skirt, signaling her amusement as she enjoyed her Flame Soda.

"Dean, the orange is perfect," Blanchet said, seated next to Pippita. She wore a paisley mini-dress with flowing sleeves and black go-go boots. Perched on Blanchet's huge afro was a small top hat.

Blanchet was a calm respite from the hotheaded Pippita, with prospects of becoming a respectable witch doctor. But Dean still hadn't fully forgiven Blanchet's part in helping Bunny deal with Fairer Than.

"Thanks, Blanchet." Dean's tone was cooler than she intended. "Pip', we need plenty of good luck with you around. You setting up my death again any time soon?"

Pippita took hold of her cloven hooves and spun on the

stool, laughing.

"Hey, you made it easy!" she said. "You *came* to the fight, din'cha?"

"I shouldn't have left town for that university trip," Blanchet said. "I can't believe you set up a death match between Dean and Fairer Than."

"It was my best scheme yet!" Pippita hooted. "Making Bunny the prize on Sweetheart's Night. The faerie thought it all legit and everyone came out to watch and lay money. But you can guess who won that betting pool!"

"You," Bunny said. She set her empty milkshake glass aside. "Because you didn't bet on Dean or Fairer Than."

"Yeah, I'd put all my money on *you*!" Pippita whooped. "I was *countin'* on the daughter of a seventh daughter to unleash heck on everyone! Aaaaand how!"

Then she quieted.

"You've been awfully calm about my li'l stunt," Pippita said suspiciously. "Biding your time, maybe? You gonna turn me into a chicken? Or something?"

"Or something," Bunny said mildly.

Dean grinned as Pippita shrank and focused on her Flame Soda. Dean hovered over Bunny, her hand resting on the counter while Bunny and her friends chatted. Lunch hour was ending, but Dean didn't mind standing over Bunny in the soda shop, forever.

Bunny rose as kids exited. Just as Dean put her arm around Bunny to walk her out, Pippita exclaimed loudly to Blanchet.

"Y'know, I only set that fight up. The only way to stop it beforehand was to make *one* of 'em walk away."

But I did try not to fight, Dean wanted to say. Instead she quickly looked at Bunny, who appeared calm, as if she'd not heard Pippita—or chose not to hear.

Dean saw Maddy's friends look her way again as they hurried out the doors.

"Been bringing gifts for Bunny, every day," one whispered to the other.

Dean ignored them. She wondered how many of her classmates had placed their bets on Fairer Than.

◆

Dean had walked Bunny to her class and was crossing the schoolyard for the machinist shop when her dad's henchmen rose from the hedge and grabbed her.

They threw her into the silk curtained box of an officious *jiao*, slammed the door shut, picked up the carrying poles, and hurried away. Jostled, Dean tried to make her escape and saw that the silk curtains were hung with garlic.

"Yeeek!" she yelled, and though none touched her, she itched at the sight. Dean sneezed repeatedly.

She was a curled up, miserable vampire when her kidnappers turned the litter over and dumped her on the ground. Dean took to her feet in the main courtyard of her family's *siheyuan*, a four-sided, walled enclosure of old, tile-roofed buildings, and loudly sneezed.

"Ah! Yu Ying! You finally here! Come-come! We have exciting family meeting!" a quavering, old male voice said.

Her ancient and evil father, Zongxiang Lingbo Zhuofan Shao Shang Yu, Golden Bloody Overlord of the One Thousand Vampire Horde, stood before her, wizened, hunched, and resplendent in his embroidered silk robes and tall black hat. He smiled, his long straggly mustache lifting as the henchmen trotted off.

"Pop, why'd you take me out of school?" Dean cried. "I'm trying to be good! Actually go to classes and stuff!"

"'Good'? 'Good'?" Shang Yu repeated, perplexed. "What kind of word is that? As first daughter and son, you need to come."

"I'm not 'first daughter,' I got three sisters ahead of me, I'm 'last daughter'!" Dean said as Shang Yu dragged her by the arm across the courtyard. He was surprisingly strong for a stiff, old reanimated corpse who could not walk but only hop. "What's this all about?"

Shang Yu shushed her as a tiny and plump woman in a sheath dress, heels, and with slicked short hair emerged from the *siheyuan's* inner courtyard gate. She dripped with long strings of pearls. Flanking her were two tall and thickly mustachioed Hussars in gold braided jackets, red capes, Hessian boots, and feather plumed shakos. Their swords clanked by their sides.

"Baroness Von Blaud, you remember my heir!" Shang Yu hailed. "The one to lead my one thousand Golden Bloody Horde!"

"Ah, yes, your 'first son,'" Baroness Von Blaud said, eying Dean through her bejeweled lorgnette.

"I'm not—" Dean said.

Shang Yu hopped directly on her foot.

After a few more exchanges of pleasantries between her father and the baroness, in which the Hussars stared balefully down at Dean, the baroness departed for the main courtyard's outer gate.

"Are you still trying to pass me off as a match for her daughter?" Dean hissed.

"Ah-ho-ho-ho! No-no! I only interested in her horses."

"Huh?" Dean said.

Her father resumed pulling her into the inner courtyard, then past the wings of their private residences for the courtyard's garden and principle building.

"Pop, what's this about?" Dean demanded as they climbed the steps for the entrance.

"It our waking time! Waking time!" Shang Yu sang gaily. "Every hundred or thousand years, it becomes *our* time." He suddenly stopped and pointed a bony and sharp-nailed finger at her. "You gonna learn what that means."

He pushed her through the doors into the principle room, where a great table had been brought in. Her father hopped quickly and with an audible crack of his spine, took the seat at the head.

Vampires young and ancient sat, though Shang Yu was the sole representation of the ancient part. The elder vampires hardly left their apartments, spent in stupor. They found it difficult to venture out and suck *qi* from the wary and savvy denizens of the Twilight World. Dean, however, sucked blood rather than life's energy, thanks to her mother, pop's sixth wife, being a vampire of the Western European variety.

"Everyone! Everyone! You stop it with the Chinese and speak English for number one son, here," Shang Yu announced to the room. "She never go to Chinese school because she such a delinquent!" Shang Yu reached over and roughed up Dean's ducktail while the people in the room laughed.

"Pop!" Dean said, indignant.

Prominent vampires sat present besides those of Shang Yu's household. The white-faced and red-robed Qing dynasty beauty, Saffron, moved her eyes flirtatiously behind her silk fan. Dean's elder sister, Yin, wore her customary black men's changshan with white cuffs and sat next to Saffron. Long, black hair in a braid, Yin looked bored and ignored Dean's greeting. Dean was certain Yin was mentally practicing gung fu. General Fao (a rank he'd bestowed upon himself) with his short haircut, pencil mustache, monocle, epaulets, and gold braid, was stuffed into his Western-style imperial uniform and sat self-importantly at the other end of the table. A handsome male vampire in a Qing era black cap and robe sat alert and ready. Dean had never learned his name.

Shang Yu himself was a mix of dynastic styles—Ming, Song, Han—but his children suspected he did so to hide his true age. For all they knew, Shang Yu (if that really was his name) might have existed since the reign of Qin Shi Huang, China's first emperor, and therefore was possibly the eldest of them all.

Dean looked across at Saffron and Yin and the display board behind them. Pinned to it was a large map of the Twilight World's Great Steppes, complete with colored flags.

That's strange. Dean identified black flags in the steppes, where black flags should not be.

"Order, order!" Shang Yu ordered. Everyone at the table quieted. "We have very important news to discuss. *Interesting* matters. Evil stirs, and we Yu clan, who generously volunteer our warriors, who are the first defense of Little Salem and these parts of Twilight World, are now made aware."

Dean suppressed her snort. There was no "first defense" in Little Salem. The Twilight World maintained an unspoken balance where any fighting rose and fell within the realms they occurred in. Yu clan's Golden Bloody Horde was on the steppes because there was nowhere else to put them.

"General of my Golden Bloody Horde," Shan Yu summoned with an authoritative finger. "You will now speak."

"Great Yu," Fao said. He rose and bowed in Shang Yu's direction. "Indeed. Do not be surprised for what I am about to share. We who protect the Great Steppes, maneuvering our Horde so that none may threaten our town and world, have eternally watched and defended! Without complaint and without alarm to our citizens. Always, we've kept peace on the steppes. But *now* something is happening."

He looked about the table in solemnity. "The Living Dead Huns are *moving*."

"Ohhh," Saffron said, clutching her fan.

A murmur of concern rose around the table.

"Moving," a man murmured to another.

"Moooving," a second said in a hushed voice.

"And?" Dean said.

"'And?'" Fao said impatiently. "I said they were moving."

"Yeah, but they're always moving, they're the Living Dead Huns!" Dean said. "Rampaging, singing, always riding, and always moving Huns! So what's new?"

"They are moving deeper *into* our steppes," Fao said. "Where they don't belong. And Horde patrols have not kept them back."

A businessman in a sloped fedora and silk suit stood up and stabbed his finger at Fao.

"You should be doing your job!" he shouted.

"Order, order!" Shang Yu said.

"That is why I'm here, to tell you that more needs to be

done," Fao said loudly. "Though we are the mighty Golden Bloody Horde, even we know to ask for aid against such rising threat. The Von Blauds pledge their Hussars. We must also seek support from Little Salem and all neighboring towns. We must not only drive the Huns back to where they came from, but deal their forces a blow they will never forget!"

"Hear, hear!" a businesswoman in a cloche hat said above the enthusiastic poundings upon the table. She brandished her long, black cigarette holder, her lip curling. Dean saw her diamond studded fang flash against her red lips.

"Have the Huns really grown into such a threat?" Dean asked, skeptical. "What happened to putting a few of their heads on warning pikes? Or to doubling up patrols?"

She glanced at Yin, who led patrols on the steppes, and waited for her sister to back up her suggestion. Instead, Yin yawned, seemingly paying the discussion no heed.

"No-no!" a portly man in a pinstriped suit said. "You have not been paying attention. Month after month, we've lost caravans crossing the steppes—to these Huns! And now this, an invasion! If Yu clan doesn't move against them, this will upset the spice merchants, who need assurance that you *will* secure their supply route through steppe's territory."

"Like as if we don't have enough pepper," Dean scoffed.

"And remember the tea merchants!" Saffron said. She giggled behind her fan.

"Yes, the tea! The tea!" came vigorous affirmations around the table.

"But we don't drink tea," Dean said.

"We are talking about tea for the *entire* Twilight World,"

the woman with the cigarette holder sniffed. "A responsibility you should remember."

"What do you control?" Dean asked. "The diamonds?"

"We let the Huns take the Great Steppes, they will take everything!" Shang Yu declared. He hit the table with his bony fist. "Oh ho-ho-ho," he weakly added, cradling the hand as if he had hurt it.

"Do not fear, great ancestor!" the man in the black cap said. His handsome face with its sharp brows was earnest. "Righteous gung fu is on our side! No Hun bandits will have a chance to advance, for we are ready with our great *qi*, which deflects swords and clubs, to defend what is ours!"

Saffron clapped enthusiastically while the others expressed their approval.

Oh brother, Dean thought.

"This is a bluff, right?" she said, incredulous. "Show them how big a Horde we got and then they back off? There's no way we're going to start a war, are we?"

"I thought you said your daughter liked a good fight," Fao said to Shang Yu.

"I think you're all talk," Dean accused. "Making up stuff to keep your job."

Fao stood angrily, his chair scraping the floor. Dean stood too.

"Ho-ho-ho-*ho*!" Shang Yu laughed. "Come, come-come. Everyone sit down. Now Yu Ying, you shut up and we gonna hear more of what General Fao has 'made up.'"

Dean sat reluctantly once Fao resumed his seat.

Fao then explained in a slow and pompous voice, as if to make clear to Dean, where and when the Huns had been attacking and gaining in steppe territory. Dean wondered:

so the Huns were encroaching, but why? But before Dean could ask, she suddenly could not speak.

Her entire body felt like separating. If she actually breathed, that vital essence was being pulled right out of her.

W-w-what —

And then her ghost was snatched away.

Disembodied, Dean did not know where she rushed to. Or how. She only knew that suddenly she was *back* — in the real world — where sunlight and shadows confused her and dirt crumbled between her clutching fingers. Her body was bigger, heavier, *hot*, and needed to —

"Hhhhghh," she inhaled, feeling living lungs expand and fill with breath that seemed to fuel the furnace within. She exhaled and inhaled again. Then again.

She was resting on her elbows, fingers dug into the earth as she stared wide-eyed up at an equally wide-eyed cat girl. A lock of jet-black hair dangled in the girl's golden eyes as she straddled Dean and held her face. Dean saw the girl's pearl-white, satin bra rise and fall from her fully unbuttoned blouse and pushed up camisole.

The cat girl sprang back, bumping the woven, wood shelter they were in. Sunlight danced through the cracks of the shuddering branches. Dean sat up and motioned with her hands, attempting to signal calmness. She noticed the shape of her fingers — larger, thicker, and *pinker* than she knew them to be.

Who am I?

"*Hssssst!*" the cat girl hissed. Then she yowled, teeth

bared and her hackles rising.

Dean immediately raised her hands in surrender.

The cat girl's gaze narrowed. She leaned cautiously, nostrils quivering. She scented the air as Dean sat motionless.

Motionless was harder to accomplish when Dean's chest kept moving in the act of breathing.

The cat girl then snorted.

"You're not you," she said, deeply disappointed. She turned away, pulling down her camisole. She began buttoning her blouse. "Whoever you are, don't look!"

Dean clapped a hand over her eyes. She accidentally smacked herself in the face by doing so.

"I'm sorry—" she said, startled by the strange, strong depth to her voice. It had a rich timbre.

But the cat girl ignored her, found her sweater and shoes, and slipped quickly out of the bower. Dean peeked through her fingers and saw the young woman in sunlight, pulling twigs from her hair. Then she was gone.

Dean put a hand to her mouth, concerned. Then she felt her mouth in surprise.

"Wow, my lips, and...wow! My chest!" She finally noticed what moved up and down. She took hold of her breasts, made heavy by a completely undone bodice. "These are..."

In realization, she clapped hands to the sides of her head. The action was like twin blows that sent her reeling. "Ow! And I'm too strong! Well, no wonder, I'm *her*! I have to show Bunny! And—I need to get back to my own body! Heck if I'll let Pop see me like this. Bunny will know what to do. But if I'm here, then—"

Dean gulped. Yu clan was a closely guarded family. Wealthy vampires were like that. Sinister vampires were like that. Pop would not like a stranger among them, listening to military plans.

She tried to re-do her bodice's fastenings. It took her a while to figure out the lacing. When she thought she was suitably dressed, Dean emerged from the bower.

And broke off half of the entrance's arch with her hand.

"Damn!" she said, staring at the snapped off branches. "I didn't mean that. I'll—I'll fix it later."

She headed quickly into the Enchanting Forest.

CHAPTER THREE
Not Dean

Fairer Than inhaled sharply, feeling far too cold and thin. She was inside a great, wood-paneled space, a cold place, and she was seated at a long table surrounded by other cold creatures.

She tensed, lip curling. Her teeth felt different.

A wizened and long-whiskered man in a tall hat sat at the head. Other very pale vampires sat around her. The fat general at the far end, with his huge epaulets and monocle, wore a ridiculous little mustache.

"What your problem now, Yu Ying?" the old man in the tall black hat demanded.

A young woman in black with white cuffs snickered across from her.

"She probably wanted to fart," she said, snide.

The other table occupants laughed, including the old man. Fairer Than saw the large map hung behind the mocking woman and her giggling neighbor, who hid her fangs behind a silk fan. The map was of the Great Steppes, the large territory pinned with flags. Fairer Than's gaze followed the black flags that clearly marked the trespass of an unknown force.

"As I was saying," the general said in irritation. "We must do everything we can to secure the steppes."

"Okay, let's be plain," the old man said. "Yeah, spices. Yeah, medicines, oil, bananas, who cares. We talking about the gold mines. Up in the Stony Mountains where all those little men are."

"You mean the dwarves," a woman in a cloche hat and with a long stemmed cigarette holder said. "They also harvest my diamonds."

"Yeah, them. They also need the steppes for their trade. I all for protecting tea, but I like the gold."

"And don't forget the silver ore!" the woman with the fan said. She giggled.

"Yes, yes! The silver mines!" came the enthused voices around the table.

"What—" Fairer Than said, then stopped. Her voice had sounded so...casual. Immature. She cleared her throat.

"What, 'what', Yu Ying?" the old vampire said.

"What are the strengths of such enemy forces?" she said with deliberate smoothness. She lent her new voice a deep tone and felt it sounded more like herself. "Have they any weaknesses?"

"Ha! Good!" the old man said, slapping the tabletop. "Now my daughter pays attention. Answer the question, General!"

"Weaknesses! Yes! Our spies have certain observations to report," the general began, puffing his chest.

Fairer Than gave his words only half her attention. The rest had their eyes on him. She looked at her hand on the table, white, slim, and long fingered like a musician's or artist's and so unlike her own, which were calloused from clearing fields for old witches and from wielding weapons. She always kept her nails clean however, and the ones of her present hand were pristine as well, nearly silvery as if they had a polish. She flexed her fingers and watched her strange, slender hand move.

I doubt this body could barely lift a house, she thought in disdain.

"We make an effective attack," the general said. "Then ensure that all retaliations are met with crushing force. The Huns would not dare to encroach again."

"Yes, yes! Effective blows, and then it's done," the old man said. "Ha! Some war it will be, eh, Yu Ying? Shorter than a holiday!"

"As you say," Fairer Than said, glancing at the map again.

"General Fao!" the old man said. "You present your plan to us! But not now, I sleepy! We reassemble in twenty-four hours!"

"If I might clarify, you mean at 1600 hours, which is four o'clock," Fao said.

"Okay! Someone wake me later! Good bye!" The old vampire rose, and hopped away.

The others stood as well and Fairer Than did so slowly, wondering at the lightness of her body. She stepped away from the table and walked for the double doors she assumed led to the outside. Attendants opened the doors for her and bowed. She stepped directly into sunlight and a garden courtyard. Her leather jacket squeaked.

Dungarees, she thought. Boots. Belt. Tee shirt. Jacket of leather and buckles.

She wanted to strip it all off, unable to recall when she'd

worn trousers last. Before she could kick off the boots, she realized her present feet might be tender. She shirked the jacket and left it on a stone bench. Red dragon carp swam in the pond, and the water gave her no reflection. When she touched her hair, she pulled her fingers away, disgusted. Her combed back hair was greasy with pomade.

"Ugh."

She was, without a doubt, *that* vampire.

"Hey," hailed the female vampire dressed in black with white cuffs.

Fairer Than nodded to her. She should have found the exit and left. The girl came by her side.

"You're being too concerned, you know that? You spend too much time with the good witches." She stared at Fairer Than. "Just play along with Pop. He does this sort of thing every hundred years or so. There's no stopping it when it gets rolling."

Fairer Than saw someone emerge from the wing of one of the surrounding buildings. It was an ancient female vampire, powder-faced and with a high wig, decorated with hanging jewels. She was a tall creature but frail and slow moving. Her hands shook. Two attendants stayed close, and one offered her birds in a golden cage. The old vampire snarled and clutched the cage. She drew the life out of the alarmed birds until they were silenced.

"Look, you're too young to know, but he makes stuff happen to keep the family lively," the girl continued. The old vampire made her trembling way across the porch. Fairer Than didn't think the vampire's meal had helped her. "The old ones got to feed on something, that means some misery and stuff. To get that, it has to be us against the Huns."

The girl slapped Fairer Than on her back. "See you at the front!"

As she turned to leave, Fairer Than spoke.

"You mean against the Living Dead Huns, who never die, but rise, over and over again?"

The girl stopped and looked at her.

"It will be glorious, yeah?" she said, grinning. She waved as she walked away.

Fairer Than saw the courtyard's gates and walked quickly for them. She entered a greater courtyard, and then approached the last pair of gates. She left the vampire compound, a hunger gnawing within her. Down the hill and past the high walls and richer estates lay the main street of Little Salem.

✦

Yin walked back into the principle house, where her father whispered orders to his henchmen. They bowed, and disappeared.

"I thought you were sleeping," Yin said.

"So you talked to First Daughter! How she doing?" Shang Yu said.

Yin rubbed her nose. "She's acting differently."

"You so young, you don't know better." Shang Yu laughed. He hopped away.

Yin shrugged. She only had one part to play in her Pop's big scheme, and since it was all she was tasked to do, she was committed to doing it well. She left to rejoin her patrol on the steppes.

✦

The bell rang, and school ended for another day. Haunt High's students poured out of its doors, windows, and clock tower. Bunny bade farewell to Blanchet and Pippita and waited at the school gates for Dean. Unlike the other departing witches, she hadn't brought her broom. After thirty minutes and some homework done, she went looking for her girlfriend. She found Dean's buddy, Danny, in the auto shop.

"Dean? Haven't seen her!" Danny said. Part vampire and devil-boy, he wiped his greasy hands off on a rag. His gaze connected with someone behind her, and Bunny turned in time to see Dean's other buddy, Cesar, motion with his thumb, a gesture resembling *get rid of something*. The greaser then turned quickly, returning his attention to an engine part.

"She skipped shop today, and that's one class she wouldn't ditch, so no, she ain't here, Bunny," Danny said. "Uh, bye!"

Then Danny turned away too. Perplexed by the boys' behavior, Bunny left. After checking the detention room, she hugged her books and walked home, wondering if Dean was elsewhere, fighting again.

In Little Salem's Main Street, irate demon bikers picked up collapsed bikes before the beauty shop. They yelled about going after somebody. Bunny caught the big leader's eye as she walked past. He gave her a look over his sunglasses.

"Never mind, let's get outta here," he yelled at his gang and gunned his bike.

He and his pack roared away, leaving Bunny bewildered. Since Sweetheart's Night, people had been quick to become scarce in her presence. She'd complained about it to Blanchet.

"Well, I'd heard that Fairer Than gave you some dragon's breath on Sweetheart's Night?" Blanchet had said. "And then people saw how powerful you could get. We all knew it was prophesied you'd be high witch someday...it's just now we *really* know."

"Why does everyone believe what a drunk seer said?" Bunny had said, incensed. "If you'd had dragon's breath, Blanchet, you'd have knocked a few trees down too."

"Maybe," Blanchet had said, "but I'm not the Baker daughter of a seventh daughter."

Bunny's aunties never made anything more of her heritage than if they'd found her as a baby in a basket or in a cabbage leaf. There were many powerful witches, warlocks, sorceress queens, and faeries in the Twilight World. Bunny felt she was one among many born under stars or portents.

"You are going to be a witch doctor," Bunny had said to her friend. "I've won ribbons for my cakes. I don't think my baking skills compare."

Which was why Fairer Than's attentions had been inexplicable since Bunny was also a mere teen—with looks inherited from her beautiful mother, yes, and she'd her mother's sensual attitude—but her level of sexiness was nothing compared to Fairer Than's. That was a power that had nearly seduced her completely.

Trying to reject Fairer Than with a kiss tainted with *Repelere* lipstick had been a foolish move on Bunny's part. Dean's anger, acceptance of a death race challenge, and then *death match* with Fairer Than had been even more foolish.

In the aftermath, she and Dean made up, but Bunny wasn't immune to the gossip and glances at school. Part-dragon beings were considered a catch, despite their reputation for being notorious seducers and heartbreakers. Even Blanchet had had to wonder.

"Dean's good to me," Bunny had told Blanchet on a walk to school.

"Um, do you remember when you two were fighting?" Blanchet had said.

"Not really," Bunny had answered, surprising herself. "That's all in the past. Can you see Fairer Than and myself lasting longer than what Dean and I have?"

"I guess not," Blanchet had admitted. "Dean *is* safer."

Bunny had to push her smirking friend for saying that.

But since the events of Sweethearts Night, Fairer Than seemed less preoccupied with seduction and more about assuaging a possible broken heart. For that, Bunny felt terrible. Especially when her aunties would chase Fairer Than away.

"She's still bad," Bunny reminded herself. "I know about the other girls."

And that, she told herself, was not her concern.

Bunny walked among the forest pines, the mossy ground dotted with white flowers and sunbeams, both of which reminded her of Fairer Than. A sapling she'd planted seemed to be thriving—one of several she'd placed in the forest, hoping to atone for the damage she'd wrought on Sweetheart's Night. After a brief detour to check on her other plantings, she entered the hollow where her home lay. Butterflies and bees flew in their cottage's front garden. Bunny gladdened. She had arrived home without incident. Right when she opened the garden's gate, someone hailed her. Honey ran down the path and waved.

"Honey," Bunny cried, rushing forwards. She rarely saw Honey, who was always on adventures.

"I found you!" Honey exclaimed when they hugged. "And guess what, I did something funny to that faerie, Fairer Than, and your girlfriend, Dean."

♦

Once she reached town, Fairer Than picked a gladiola and put it in her hair. She tied up her tee shirt, exposing her midriff, and felt only barely womanly, for her hips did not sway as she liked. She walked through the centre of Little Salem, ignored pangs at the drifting scent of Blood Burgers grilling at Shivers, saw none of her reflections in store windows, and elicited a few sneers and catcalls from demon bikers loitering before the corner drugstore. Her senses felt as halved as her present body weight. She did not view trees and plants as she'd known them, vibrant and whispering with life, nor did the sun feel very appealing on her skin or pretty to her sight. She was cold and motionless inside, and she had no breath in her to even muster.

"What wretchedness!" she muttered. "How can one exist like this?"

What irritated her most was her persistent hunger.

"Hey, Dean," a skull girl called from the beautician shop, her tone surprised.

A devil girl came to stand next to the skull girl and looked Fairer Than up and down.

"Hey, Dean," said the devil girl expectantly.

"Ladies," Fairer Than said to them as she passed, her

mouth's corner curling into a grin, and thought the devil girl looked tasty. She swayed more for good measure, and the girls giggled.

"Dean!" yelled a burly demon biker in a spiked helmet. He rode his rumbling bike along side her.

He was one of the gang from the drugstore, and Fairer Than assumed by his size that he was the leader. "What's with the girly act? You lose a bet, or something?"

His buddies pulled their bikes alongside his and laughed.

"Indeed, it was something," Fairer Than said.

She decided to forestall any escalating, crude remarks. She kicked out and tipped the burly biker into the bikes of his buddies. The ones caught in the domino effect went down with a loud crash. Fairer Than then ducked into Amplithuhedron's Book Swarm, hurried past the book stacks, and ran out the back door. Were she in her original form, she would have remained and trounced the bikers. But since she was presently a mere vampire, she ran until she left Little Salem proper for the woods. No sound of pursuing bikes followed.

The forest, like the trees and flowers of town, did not speak to her. The pines and bushes were silent, distant, and almost foreboding. Sunlight and shadow played on the forest floor as she ran. Birds and tiny animals took swift flight before her, seemingly eager to not be in her company. She felt separated from true life and more like a furtive shade, borrowing time with earth and sky.

A rabbit bounded for the bushes and disappeared. To her dismay, her only reaction to its presence was a sudden desire to bite it and suck it dry.

"Truly, vampires are cursed!" she exclaimed.

Like it or not, she would have to go to Bunny. She could

only determine that her body-switch had something to do with the enchanted sugar Bunny's cousin had flung. It was not a state she wanted Bunny to see her in. Being transformed into a frog would have been better. Or even a rock. Going to Bunny in the form of her beloved was a cruel joke to them both.

Fairer Than emerged from the woods for The Lady's Lake, which lay placid and blue. Following the shore, she tried to calm, a hand laid on her woefully flat chest. The heart there did not beat, but a heart was present. Was it the cause of her upset? She seemed too affected by her present circumstance thanks, perhaps, to the organ's presence. Such depth of emotion was unfamiliar.

For when she'd found that her first and last wife had died while she'd been away on the First Crusade, Fairer Than had fallen into a rare state of being: melancholy. At least, she remembered it as possibly being thus. That was when she hid her heart. She had placed it in a goose egg, locked it within a sealed chest, and entrusted it to the sister of Mab and the equal of Titania, the Lady of the Lake.

She recalled that long ago time. When she'd summoned Lady from her watery home, the faerie had taken in Fairer Than's appearance with curiosity. It was rare to find Fairer Than in male form.

"Thy beard suits," Lady had observed.

"By my dead wife's naming I was known to the world as 'Handsome,'" Fairer Than had said. "Handsome shall be no more."

She considered Lady the most sympathetic of her faerie kin and perhaps the only one she could trust. Lady had accepted her heart and hidden it beneath a man-eating maelstrom. Fairer Than returned to the forest, leaving behind her surviving children, the grave of her wife, and the world of mortal men. She took the form of a woman ever then.

Fairer Than, hands on her narrow hips, stared out at the water. Bunny's home was a short distance away.

"Are you there, Lady? 'Tis I, Fairer Than," she called.

She watched the water. Even the water maidens did not bother to raise their heads.

Why summon the Lady of the Lake? There were other beings she could consult—for a price—to reverse the switching spell. She doubted she was seeking a fellow faerie for a philosophical discussion about Love. But she did wish to express her frustration to one who would *know*. Fairer Than the Fairest was, after so many centuries, making a fool of herself over a witch again.

"And thrice a fool! I can't speak to Lady in this form."

Requesting the Lady come before a bloodsucking creature (and one with such foul hair) was a significant breach of etiquette.

"Forgive me, I'll return anon when I'm myself again," she promised, and promptly left the lakeside.

After fleeing the Dog & Whistle, Honey found Little Salem's Main Street, but made no further progress reaching Bunny's cottage, despite asking for directions at the barbershop, corner drugstore, and magazine stand. She saw the soda shop, Shivers, once, but misplaced it the moment it was out of view, despite smelling its burgers frying. Since circumstances deigned that she should dally in town, she made the best of things by grabbing an afternoon meal.

She took a stool at Julio's Devil Sauce Fish Tacos Stand and ordered.

Once served, she squeezed the lime slice over her piping hot grilled fish tacos with roasted corn, salsa, and a side of Devil Sauce. She looked out at Main Street as passerby shopped, walked, loitered, and gossiped. Under the sun and blue skies, it was an idyllic scene. Little Salem was well-to-do, comfortable, and beautiful, just like Silverdale. But fear would be the easiest way to undermine it. She tried to imagine the same street under such rule, like some dismal towns she'd seen, weighed by taxes, an iron hand, and sucked dry by greed.

"Oh, hot," she said, waving a hand before her mouth. She liked spicy foods, but it took some getting used to. She swallowed a huge draught of her orange drink.

Meal finished, Honey attended to something that had been on her mind since her run-in with Fairer Than. She entered a telephone booth next to the taco stand, dropped nickels in the slot, and dialed Dr. Sugar Baker's extension at the university where she taught. Her sister, thankfully, was in her office and picked up. Honey asked her about the spell she'd cast on Fairer Than.

"Sweetheart," Sugar said reassuringly. "It's simply meant for body-swappin'."

Sugar drawled like she was raised amongst the humans in the American South, and she was. Sometimes kin journeyed beyond the protective mists of the Twilight World in search of something more or something missing. Sometimes kin was chosen to go beyond the veiled seas, for whatever reason foretold. Sugar was one of those, and as a child left to make her way in the greater world. Once grown, she returned to the Twilight World. Like many who had traveled beyond and managed to come back, she valued the sanctuary of their reality.

"Ah could've made it a simple teleportation spell," Sugar then said. "But it seemed more in your favor to have people confused. The spell switches your target with his or her opposite, or more aptly, the person's opponent. Considerin' that you deal with political types most times, Hon'—"

"Yes?" Honey said.

"I figured a transposition would rock things a li'l."

It sure would, if the spell had worked on the dragon-faerie. Hanging up, she set out once more.

"Julio said Bunny's house was this way." Honey made her way to the lake and to its shore. "Follow the shore west. Until I come to a—oh! A vampire!"

An androgynous vampire in dungarees and motorcycle boots stood at the shore's edge, palms out as if to summon someone or something. But Honey didn't believe the vampire was supplicating. The ease with which the figure stood, erect, proud, and gaze forwards, looked more like a pose of command. The vampire abruptly abandoned the pose and turned, noticing Honey.

The vampire was a "she"—whether of the boy or girl variety, Honey wasn't sure. The vampire approached with swaying hips and bared midriff. A gladiola flower was in her slicked back, duck-tailed hair. Her eyelids were heavy and her mouth pursed. She looked at Honey and Honey felt like she'd seen that smoldering gaze before.

"I'm having a difficult time with this body," the vampire stated when she neared. "It's thin, needs hips, and has no breasts."

"Oh, I don't know, I think I see some." Honey looked. "Breasts, I mean. So...do I know you?"

"Not in this body, you do not." The vampire sniffed. "As Bunny's cousin, are you not familiar with her beau? Not long ago, *you* flung enchanted sugar at *me* in the Dog & Whistle."

Honey covered her mouth. "Oh my goodness! You're that dragon-thing! And now you're *Dean*?"

Fairer Than's lip curled. "A vampire's body is a wretched state to be trapped in. Apparently, Bunny's beau harbors a constant craving for the coursing blood in girls like you."

"Oh?" Honey reached for her wand—then couldn't recall where she'd put it. "Wait, that might just be *you*. Vampires are trained for that hunger, or they're exiled from the Twilight World."

"Or beheaded," Fairer Than said, seemingly relishing the thought.

"Just keep your cravings to yourself!"

"Do you live so far away that you have not yet met this form?"

"I'm often on missions," Honey said.

"Missions," Fairer Than repeated. Her head tilted as if considering the implication. "You had said an odd thing at the Dog and Whistle…about how you thought I should have killed the vampire."

"I'm not explaining anything to you," Honey said defensively. "Not until I see Bunny. And—don't behead yourself. You need to take care of that body."

Fairer Than shifted her weight to her other hip, laid a hand on it, and then placed one in her hair. "I don't know what Bunny sees in this lacking form."

"Sometimes it's not the body that interests us, Fairer Than, it's the person. We need to go to Bunny's house. Do you know the way?"

"It is there." Fairer Than pointed over Honey's shoulder. Honey looked behind and saw a faraway chimney's smoke, drifting above the trees. Honey estimated that the cottage was, at most, a seven-minute walk.

"It's just like me to pass it," she said.

"Instead of going there, why not reverse the spell now?" Fairer Than demanded.

"Bunny is more powerful. She's a daughter of a seventh daughter, did you know? Compared to her, I'm not so great. I might mess up again."

"Very well." Fairer Than sighed, looking unhappy. "I knew that about her. Let us go."

She motioned towards a path, and Honey eagerly led.

Just as Honey entered the forest, a tussle sounded behind her. Two large men grabbed Fairer Than and tossed her into a litter's ornate box.

"Argh! What is this garlic doing to me?" Fairer Than exclaimed as the men shut the door. They picked up the litter by its poles and ran down the shore.

"*Hey!*" Honey ran after them. "I need her! Bring her back!"

The men and their litter disappeared into the woods.

"Great!" Honey exclaimed. "If I try to follow—"

She halted. She knew very well that was something she shouldn't attempt.

Sometimes her gift was a burden. She hurt most when faced with a kidnapping—or when having promised to return to a sweet shepherd or handsome woodsman, knowing she'd never find that person again.

She clutched her chest.

"Whoa. That hurt. Don't do that to yourself, Honey."

When her heart's pang passed, Honey set her jaw and looked for the distant smoke of Bunny's chimney.

CHAPTER FOUR
Mightier Than Faerie

Dean didn't understand forests, and therefore could never find her way in them.

Trees, bushes, rocks; they all looked the same to her, whereas Bunny knew the woods with great knowledge and fondness. Dean had never spent time with faerie-kin, whether sprites or even the water maidens Bunny spoke of. Creatures of the earth and nature usually shunned vampires. But Fairer Than's body gave Dean extra senses that she recognized could lead her where she may wish to go, merely by taking in the forest life and understanding what it told her.

She wandered, amazed by the way sunlight streamed and somehow made a soft sound. The trees hummed, and so did the pungent earth, at a lower, sonorous tone. Life was everywhere on the colorful forest floor and in the branches above, revealing tiny faerie folk, insects, reptiles, and furry animals, busy at their business or merely lurking. To her surprise, none ran away. They either ignored her presence or at least tipped a flower hat in her direction. Dark faeries with malevolent faces stared back at her, and then rendered themselves part of their surroundings.

Dean wondered how she'd missed noticing all such little creatures before.

Is this 'faerie sight'? Can Bunny see the forest like this too?

She stopped to take a deep breath and threw her arms out, her chest expanding. A vigor thrummed through her entire being that she could only attribute to living blood rushing through muscles and activating cells that sucked in oxygen with her. Curious birds alighted and looked down from branches, twittering.

"Hey!" she said with a broad smile, pointing at them. She then looked down at herself, admiring Fairer Than's shapely proportions and hips. She touched the heavy, gold belt that hung at her pelvis and peered at the strung canines. The belt's dangling end terminated with a curious ornament. Picking it up, she studied it. It was a shard embedded in gold and shaped like the snapped-off tip to a flat, pointed blade.

"It's a scale!" Dean watched the scale's surface become iridescent in the sunlight. "A fish's? A lizard's? That's one giant lizard!"

She touched the scale. It sliced her finger. She quickly stuck the wound in her mouth.

Automatically, she sucked on it, only to discover that the wound had rapidly closed. She pulled the finger from her lips to look at the healing scar. Though she'd just tasted blood, she had no desire to have more.

"Ha!" she laughed in surprise. "*Ha-ha!*"

The birds flew off as Dean yelled to the treetops.

"*Yeah!*" she cried.

She bop a doo-wop

Dean resumed her passage into the forest, a spring to her

step. She gave the thumbs up sign to every little creature she saw, even industrious beetles. When she happened on a fork in the path, she stopped and regarded the gnarled oak that stood between the two destinations.

"What if I said: show me the way to the Baker cottage, honorable tree?" she asked the tree.

She watched the oak rustle. A large branch bent gently over the left path.

"Thanks!" Dean said, and strolled down the path indicated.

A *shang-a-lang a doo wow*

But something tugged at her to step off the path.

Dean shrugged the sensation away and continued.

The silent summons repeated.

What is that?

Whatever was calling couldn't be heard, only known. The invitation gave a signal she could follow like the knowing walk that lent movement to a girl's beckoning behind.

Dean stepped off the path.

She followed the summons's call and arrived at a large hollow, one with sunlight streaming upon a ring of mushrooms. She stepped towards them and felt herself pass through a shimmering veil.

Fireflies hovered and twinkled in the dark parts of the trees. Small brownies and hobgoblins hurriedly set food and drink on a long banquet table. Underfoot were tiny, winged faeries who cavorted amongst the mushroom caps and clover. Some rode about on snails, enticing their steeds with dangling strawberries. Others raced dragonflies, swooping through the air around Dean's head. One sprite stood upon a white rabbit and beat it with a twig.

Dean plucked the fellow off, tossed him, and picked up the rabbit. It was warm and trusting in her hand. Delighted to finally touch an animal that didn't flee, she nuzzled it.

"Go there! There! Big feet!" a brownie exclaimed at her feet. He balanced a small jug on his head and pointed imperiously at a fallen tree trunk on the edge of the clearing.

"I was just leaving," Dean said, though she moved for the tree trunk to appease the impatient brownie prodding her with his foot.

When she was about to step out of the clearing, she saw others enter, passing like spirits through the cloaking veil. Once in the sunlight, they became whole; nymphs in gossamer raiment, elves in the greens and browns of the forest, and a bearded merman draped in seaweed. Dean saw a sylph alight from above. They mingled, laughed, and partook of the table's offerings. A girl wearing a seashell-decorated crown and with long, dark hair to her buttocks stood with her back to Dean, conversing with a blonde dryad. The dark-haired faerie was nude, but the blonde had wreaths of ivy wrapped around her person.

And when a diminutive band of insects, led by a frog in a tailcoat and spectacles, began to play, the faeries moved to dance.

Enchanted, Dean sat down on the tree trunk, the bunny in her lap, and watched.

A vampire's ball has nothing on this.

She noticed the dark ones lurking among the revelers, malevolent-faced imps, goblins, and silent, wet creatures who made her think of drownings. But she sensed, like the Twilight World as a whole, that the representation of faerie seemed a balance. There was present a great many whose countenances held no ill will or intent. Dean could not say that vampires who gathered inspired the same.

Go to a vampire ball and it's all shadows. Cold creatures dwelling in the dark.

"Will she announce that we withdraw and hide ourselves, once again?" the merman said to one of the elves. "The Twilight World is our haven."

The elf opened his slender hands. "Our queen knows best the signs of trouble."

What trouble? Do they know about the Huns? Dean petted the rabbit, wondering if she should stay to learn more. A pretty faerie draped in flowers danced near. She laid a hand on Dean's cheek with familiarity and looked at her with bright-eyed expectancy.

"Thou will not kiss me?" she said, pouting.

"Another time," Dean said, smiling.

"Oh, and won't thou kiss me?" a smiling faerie asked, suddenly drawing near.

"Another time," the first girl said with ill temper, and pushed the other faerie away.

They did not linger, but Dean was uplifted by their brief visit. Right then, she could not summon any aspect within herself that could be called vampirism. She had no desire, whatsoever, to find out what the blood of a faerie tasted like.

"Thou hast a most manic grin!" a faerie clothed in fluttering fabrics said as she floated by. Her words were soft like a breeze.

"Just had a happy thought," Dean said gaily. "No fangs to see, right?"

The faerie cocked her head.

"None," she whispered. "Though the winds did tell us

of what shall come. We had suspected thy warrior countenance, in that spirit, had returned."

"My what?" Dean said, as the faerie drifted away.

Dean's good mood faded like the cloud faerie's presence. She remembered Fairer Than's great longsword from their challenge fight.

Yeah, and I'm supposed to be the killer.

She wondered how Fairer Than earned the teeth on her belt.

Yin had teased her once, about being a vampire born into the Twilight World. All such vampires went to school to learn how to control their thirst. She wasn't sure if her elder sisters, made in the world outside but also blood drinkers, ever bothered to take a class. Yin solved her thirst by volunteering for patrol out on the steppes.

"Sure, you know how it feels, drinking all that life—" Yin had said to her once.

"Hey," Dean had said.

"And then the life go out of their eyes—"

"Quit it," Dean had threatened.

"You're such a baby." Yin had laughed.

Dean didn't like that kind of talk. Everyone kept to the Twilight World's rule, whether they were demons, werewolves, devils, ghosts, or faeries. Challenge fights aside, no one went about murdering each other. She'd watched her fading elders suck *qi* from plants and little animals and still thought they could try switching to buying blood, or something.

Bunny shouldn't see stuff like that.

Dean felt her time was up. She couldn't hide in Fairer Than's body forever. She was about to rise when a tiny green grasshopper in a frock coat bounded into the gathering. He brandished his fiddler's bow in her direction. Two faerie men entered the hollow, looked at the grasshopper, and then looked at Dean. Both wore leggings and embroidered velvet, and one wore a floppy hat with arcing plume. Both had identical, insolent expressions.

Hell.

The men sauntered towards her.

"For our queen, we took upon the task," the hatless one said, "to usher thee, Fairer Than Whomever, to her presence. But here thou art at her very gathering! Did thy little witch finally release thee?"

"Aye, from salubrious pastimes?" the male in the floppy hat added. They both laughed, and the female faeries around them giggled, tinkling.

Dean's gaze narrowed. She didn't know what *salubrious* meant, but she could guess.

"No doubt, thou misses thy mortal mistress," the first man grinned, leaning. "If it so comforts thee, do continue giving tonic effect to thy *bunny.*"

Dean put the rabbit down and gently urged it to return to the forest.

"You shouldn't insult witches," she said. "Or make stuff up."

The men looked offended.

"We only relate what's true," the one in the floppy hat said. But his tone was disingenuous.

"You faeries," Dean said, standing. The men nearly stepped back, and then held their ground. "You know what's true?"

"What?" the first male said, chin raised.

"This," Dean said, and punched the man on his chin.

♦

"So you're saying that Dean and Fairer Than have body-switched," Bunny said anxiously as she led Honey into the cottage.

"Unless Dean was pulling a really elaborate joke, yeah, I'm certain that was Fairer Than," Honey said. "Are the aunties in?" She raised a hand to call.

"Shh!" Bunny bade, putting Honey's hand down. "It's nap time for Aunt Hauntie and Weirdie. Aunt Agoosta might be out to market. Let's not wake them."

Honey followed her cousin up to her bedroom, trying not to make the steps creak.

Once in Bunny's room, which faced west and brought in the warm, afternoon sun, Bunny went to her pink princess phone by the open window, picked up the receiver, and dialed a number.

"Who're you calling?" Honey asked curiously.

"Dean. Or Fairer Than as Dean. Dean must have been taken home, and if she, or Fairer Than, is in her room, that's where I'm calling."

Honey nearly asked why Bunny didn't summon Dean using a scrying ball instead. Then she remembered that vampires didn't cast a reflection.

On the sunlit nightstand by Bunny's bed, a small picture frame sat, and Honey picked it up. In it was a piece of paper with cursive letters that simply said, "Dean." She put the frame back, wondering how vampires managed to do their hair or put on make-up when they couldn't see themselves.

"You're really sweet on Dean, huh?" Honey said. "She

is pretty cute."

"She is." Bunny smiled as she listened patiently to her phone.

"I can't believe I haven't met her until now." Honey reached over and repositioned the worn, stuffed toy rabbit on her cousin's bed. "But then, I still didn't really meet her, so never mind. Let me guess what she's like: sweet, lots of fun, considerate most times, makes you laugh, yet is bad and dangerous, and loves you lots?"

Bunny smiled as her fingers twirled the phone cord.

"Kind of like a puppy?"

Bunny looked askance at her.

"Puppies are no harm to the world," Honey mused. "Unless they grow up to be that."

Bunny covered the phone's receiver, her expression baffled.

"Honey, you don't usually just...visit. Was there a message you needed to deliver?"

"Yes. To you, but you should take care of Dean first."

Bunny nodded and returned her attention to her phone.

"Fairer Than, however," Honey pondered, "she's never been a puppy."

Bunny glanced her way again.

"Probably came bursting out of the Goddess's uterus like a team of horses." Honey thought about Fairer Than in the tavern. "Fire-breathing horses. If she really likes you, though, I bet she's a nice horse. But you know what I didn't expect? That she can be funny. I overheard a story she told that was hilarious. And I mean not in a way that makes fun of you. Which all faeries like to do."

"Yes...Fairer Than can be funny." Bunny smiled. "She told me once that a song she'd sung was written by a frog."

Bunny gave a breathy laugh, and then stopped herself.
She bit her lip and turned back to her phone.

Honey watched Bunny's back as her cousin listened to
the receiver.

"Well, if she ever tells you her milkmaid story, I hope
you like your jokes bawdy," Honey said.

Bunny hung up the phone. After twenty rings, she
doubted Dean would answer. She retrieved her broom.

"I should go to her house," Bunny said.

"Have you ever been?" Honey asked, curious. "Is it full
of vampires?"

Bunny sighed. She put her broom back.

"Yes. And no, I've never been. Dean preferred I never
visit—because of it being full of ancient vampires, who
aren't so nice."

Honey nodded. "Ancient mummies, ancient witches.
They're the ones to watch out for."

Bunny picked up her phone receiver again.

"I need a glass of milk," Honey said. She went to the
door. "Do you want some?"

"No thanks," Bunny said in distraction as she dialed
again. She listened to Dean's phone ring once more and
vaguely heard the bluebells tinkle in the garden; the bluebells she and her aunties had planted to warn them if faeries were near the cottage.

Dean punched the male faerie, holding back nearly all

of Fairer Than's strength. She'd been on the receiving end of Fairer Than's light taps enough to know that the dark faerie handled confrontations with a knowledgeable, watchful hand. But Dean was an eager fighter rather than a dispassionate one.

A cloud of flying, tiny faeries descended, shrieking and wielding sharp pins, and she waved them off with a little more force than necessary. The male faeries pulled long knives and Dean tapped each man in the chin once more, and then tossed the hapless men into the crowd. A frost faerie gestured, and Dean shattered the oncoming ice with a punch. Another summoned winds to knock her down, and a third caused snaking vines to rise and entangle her.

Dean snapped the vines easily, leapt to her feet, and grabbed up a giant hedgehog in a silk vest. She bowled the fellow into a group of dwarves who advanced with short swords and knocked them all down.

"The Queen!" someone cried, and horns sounded. A cadre of colorfully dressed, longhaired faerie men rushed into the hollow and towards Dean, swords drawn. She hefted the banquet table, hurled it, and then fled, bursting through the veil for the forest proper.

If Dean thought she had excellent vampiric speed, Fairer Than was faster. The moment she returned to the correct forest path, she sped to where Bunny's home lay.

Dean ran through the front gate and up the path, the bluebells tinkling madly in her wake. When she was about to knock, she felt a sharp pain on the top of her head.

"Ow!" The pain repeated, a hammer pinging. "Ow! What—?"

She looked up and saw the nailed horseshoe. Dean grabbed the door handle. She quickly stepped in, shut the door, and felt the pain in her skull lessen.

"Aunties! Stay up here. I'll take care of this," Bunny's voice said from the stairway.

Bunny hurried down the stairs and came to a halt at the sight of Dean. Bunny had a tight, warm glow surrounding her, shining white gold. Dean blinked, then stared again.

What must I look like?

"Fairer Than?" Bunny gripped her wand.

"Bunny, it's me!" Dean said.

She stepped forwards. When Bunny pointed her wand, Dean stopped.

"You're...different," Bunny said warily.

"That's because I'm Dean!"

Alarmed, Bunny descended and stood before her. Her gaze looked up to search her face. She raised a hand as if to touch her, then stopped.

"So it's true. Honey said this might happen."

"'Honey'?"

"My cousin, Honey. She'd cast a spell on Fairer Than. Then, she said she met Fairer Than, in *your* body—"

"And now I'm a faerie!" Dean exclaimed. "So it's a spell gone awry, huh?"

"Well, with Honey, 'awry' often means something more. We just don't know what, yet. Dean, were you in another fight?"

Dean looked at her in surprise. "What makes you think I was in one? I fought Fairer Than myself and it's hard to lay a finger on her."

Bunny gave a wry look. "She liked looking disheveled, but I doubt she'd ever allow something or someone to scratch her face."

"Hell." Dean touched her cheek and recalled the wee

faeries with their sword needles. "Yeah, the faeries started something, but I finished it. Wasn't hard when it feels like I can lift buildings! I mean, look at *these!*" She flexed both arms and felt her bicep swell against her armlet. She then gestured to her bosom. "This body is amazing!"

"Oh, it is." Bunny smiled. "I need to get Honey." She reached for Dean's face and gave her a quick smooch. "Don't move."

"Okay," Dean said.

Bunny left the room for the kitchen. "Honey," she called.

Dean stood still, breathing deeply.

"She took that okay."

She wondered if she could ever kiss Fairer Than as casually if Bunny were in the faerie's body. The thought made her cheeks warm and she touched them. She felt she might be blushing. Despite the embarrassment that accompanied such a physical trigger, the heat was a pleasant sensation.

The stairs creaked. Weirdette stood on the step, staring with enormous eyes. Wizened and tiny, with black hair like straw and a puckered mouth with a jutting tooth, she was as skinny and bird-like as her shriveled and grizzled sister, Hauntette, seemed sturdy—Hauntette, who squinted like a sailor, had an immense chin full of warts, and sported a peg leg. Dean saw that the life-glow around Weirdette's body was more subtle and darker, like aged wine.

So that's what 'elderly' looks like.

Weirdette ran back up the stairs as fast as her bony legs could move.

"Honey?" Bunny said, emerging from the kitchen. She went to the stairs and ran up too.

"Bunny, um," Dean said as Bunny disappeared. Bunny then spoke, muted, possibly addressing her aunts.

A plump, honey-haired girl hurried into the room from the back garden door with a glass of milk.

"Bunny?" she said. She stopped before Dean with a start.

"Bunny went, uh," Dean said, wondering who the pretty witch was, though she suspected. The witch's body-glow was as bright as Bunny's but more a yellow-gold.

"You're different," Honey said, suspicious. "So you're not back, are you?"

"Huh? I'm not Fairer Than." Dean quickly held her hands up. Honey might try defending herself. "And you're...?"

"And you're?" Honey demanded instead.

"I'm Dean! Bunny's—"

"So *you're* Dean," Honey said pensively.

"I don't look it right now, but yeah," Dean said.

"In my line of work, I meet a lot of princes." Honey quickly quaffed her milk, and then set the glass on a table. "Really nice ones, too. Until they get their heads chopped off."

"They what?" Dean said.

"The first time I lost a guy like that was really upsetting, but I've come to accept it. Maybe Bunny will, too." Honey wore a milk mustache.

"What is your line of work?" Dean asked, baffled.

"I have to find Bunny." Honey went to the cellar door, opened it, and then descended.

"But Bunny, she's," Dean said belatedly as the cellar door slammed shut.

Bunny hurried down the stairs.

"I think your cousin is in the cellar," Dean said.

"Honey does things like that." Bunny went to the cellar door. "We'll be right back."

When the cellar door closed behind Bunny, Dean looked down at herself. Was that hunger coming from her middle? It seemed a more pleasant sensation than blood-thirst. Though Fairer Than was built like a brick house, perhaps food similar to what she saw at the faerie banquet would assuage: mist cakes, dewdrops, and berries.

"If this is going to take a while, I could try eating." The thought cheered her. "Real vegetarian, 'nothing killed' eating. Maybe a peach pie."

She considered going to the kitchen. As a vampire, she'd briefly been inside the Baker cottage only to be chased out again. However, at that moment she was as warm-blooded and alive as the occupants, a being who could fit right in. Her heart swelled at the thought.

She walked to the kitchen.

A horseshoe suddenly dangled before her.

Hauntette and Weirdette stood on the stairs, holding the long, arcing fishing pole that was dangling the horseshoe. Dean quickly raised a hand in salutation.

"Goodie Bakers!" Dean hailed. "Don't mean to startle you, I'm—I'm not—"

Her skin started to crawl. Her head pounded. She suddenly experienced a flush that didn't feel good at all.

Bunny's aunties bumped the horseshoe against Dean's substantial chest. It thudded.

"Argh," Dean said as she began to itch all over. "Horseshoe!"

She turned, opened the front door, and ran out of the house. With a whoop of glee, the aunties ran down the stairs to chase her.

"Hee-hee-hee!" they cried. "Take that, you noisome faerie!"

Dean ran out the garden gate and down the path, frantically trying to recall where the lake was so she could jump in.

For as long as she could remember, Fairer Than fought her allergy to iron, a weakness she inherited from her faerie sire. When the keen desire to handle iron weaponry outweighed her aversion, she built resilience to the metal's debilitating effect. The only exception to her hard won immunity was horseshoes. Faced then with the threat of the garlic hanging around her, she called upon internal fortitude and marshaled what will her vampire body had.

She punched out the roof of the litter.

Her arm caught in the lacquered wood, failing to make the sizable hole she'd expected. She tore swiftly with the other hand to create that hole. The henchmen dropped the litter while Fairer Than extricated herself from the roof. They'd traveled into the upper neighborhood where the richer residents of Little Salem resided. Fairer Than scrambled for the street and ran. Something looped around her neck—a lasso. It was strung garlic.

"ACHOO!" Fairer Than sneezed.

As she slowed to sneeze more, a henchman ran up from behind.

She expected the blow to her head—

She hadn't expected it to ring so hard.

When she came to, her first thought was that her present, aching skull had the embarrassing resilience of porcelain. Fairer Than reluctantly opened her eyes.

She lay in a metal cage, tall enough to stand in. The cage appeared to be in a basement, and thin light shown from a lone, barred window high above. The place was very similar to dungeons. The old vampire from the meeting stood clutching the cage bars. He peered at her.

"So! Did you have to destroy my *jiao*? They not cheap, you know!"

Fairer Than rubbed the back of her head as she squinted at the old man. Though she had lived long by mortal standards, she was still very young when compared to her faerie and dragon elders. She suspected the wizened vampire before her was far older than she could suspect. He smelled of dust and death.

"You got anything to say for yourself?" the vampire demanded.

Fairer Than slowly sat up and rested her elbows on her knees.

"No," she simply said.

"Ha! Who speaks from my daughter's body?"

"The subject of a cruel joke." Fairer Than was not surprised that the old vampire knew she was a stranger in his daughter's form. "Made more so by the fact that this joke is entirely an accident."

The old vampire peered, his eyes pinpoints of black in his white face.

"My guys say you meet with a witch! Is this what the Huns are resorting to, eh? Witchcraft?"

"The Huns are wily, but this sort of spying is beyond them. You would know that."

"Heh-heh-heh!" The old vampire smiled. "And how come *you* know that?"

"They are the Living Dead Huns. Why do they enter the

steppes now?"

"I almost like you, whoever you are," the old vampire said, ignoring her question. "You stay here, we be right back."

Fairer Than watched the old vampire hop away, his henchmen following. They then carried him up the long, narrow stairs that led to the heavy prison door above. Once through, the door slammed shut. Fairer Than stood.

She turned around. Symbols were painted on the walls and ceiling.

Protection against outside spell work.

It was a proper prison, and a familiar scenario.

The memory of war horns blowing, rose. The stenches of the battlefield—of blood, stink, and death—returned once more.

"I would not have left you, Brienne," she said softly. "I was conscripted. No man the size and strength of Handsome could avoid it. But you knew better. I loved the sword, and I loved war. But no more."

Fairer Than sat again and closed her eyes. Her thirst for blood aggravated. She dwelled instead on Bunny, living in a Little Salem free of war's pall.

Having left Bunny's aunts behind in the forest, Dean ran into the lake and waded out, submerging her itching, burning self. Her feet hit a huge rock, the tip of which peeped from the water's surface. She climbed it and stepped off, then promptly sank like a two-ton weight.

Whoa! She rapidly descended and hit the sandy bottom. Having tried to punch Fairer Than, she recalled the faerie's solidity. Such density seemed inexplicable in a female, even one of Fairer Than's build, but mass times gravity equaled weight so *hey*!

She exhaled bubbles. One of her test cheats written on her hand had made her remember stuff after all. Dean pushed off and scrambled up the rock's shelf to emerge into light and air. She sat on the submerged portion, remaining head and shoulders above the water, and sighed.

Then something within her perked.

It was like the feeling she got when another vampire was near. She was not alone.

The heads of women slowly emerged from the lake's surface and regarded her.

The Daughters of the Water. They all bore the same pretty faces and long, flowing tresses. Some had a sprinkling of tiny, white flowers in their hair. Dean thought they all might be naked. As they glided closer, they whispered.

"She," one softly said.

"She," another repeated.

"Yet she is not the same."

"Witchcraft?" said another.

"*Bespell'd*. Yet does it matter?"

The one who spoke last rose higher than the rest, her breasts showing. But Dean saw the ire in her face as she addressed her sisters.

"Might it be an aspect of her, unknown 'til now, yet gives the truth of her violent nature?"

"What are you talking about?" Dean said.

The water faerie looked at her, her gaze hurt and accusing. She brought up her arm. In her dripping hand was a broken, shell-encrusted crown.

"Thou struck me for no reason," she said.

Dean's heart dropped. Horror drove a deep pit into her

stomach.

I don't fight girls.

And neither did Fairer Than. That much had come out during their challenge fight. But she couldn't recall whom she knocked down during her gleeful melee in the hollow.

The one with the broken crown sank and withdrew. Her sisters glided near and swam around Dean. She heard their soft words like running water.

"Dangerous thou were, but reigned in was thy power."

"If thou harmed, 'twas by the wickedness of thy ardor."

"Yet now, thou hast hurt us—"

"Frightened us—"

"*Angered* us."

"I didn't mean...I was just..." Dean said.

The water faeries slowly submerged and disappeared.

"I'm sorry," Dean whispered.

Bunny and Honey hurried up from the cellar and returned to the living room.

They found the front door ajar and the cottage empty. Bunny donned her pointed hat and fetched her broom, but Honey stayed her.

"Let me contact Sugar again," she urged. "Even if you find Dean, we still need to figure out how to switch them back. I bet there's a way without having both Fairer Than and Dean here. And it would be faster than chasing them."

Bunny laid her broom by the door. "You're right. The spell can be reversed remotely. I can guess how, but consult Sugar first."

Bunny then left to call for Dean in case she was hiding

nearby, while Honey sat before the dining table's scrying ball and summoned Sugar.

When Bunny returned, no Dean found, Honey had just ended her conversation with Sugar, who was about to rush out her office door to give a lecture in Extragalactic Astrophysics.

"Okay." Honey held her opened pocket diary up, its retractable chain taut. "I know how the spell should be done. Sugar says we don't have to have either Fairer Than or her body here with us to reverse the spell. We just need something of hers. Like a shoe."

"Fairer Than doesn't wear shoes."

"That's right," Honey said. She let the diary go and it retracted back to her belt.

"I have something," Bunny said. She ran upstairs.

When she came back down, she held a small cloth doll and showed it to Honey. The doll had red yarn hair, heavy-lidded eyes drawn with a wax pencil, painted green irises, big red lips also drawn in wax, and an hourglass body in a fitted green dress. Its little feet were bare.

"Aunt Weirdie and Hauntie made it with strands of Fairer Than's hair sewn into the head and a scrap of her clothing patched into the doll's dress. They were going to try a hex on it to stop Fairer Than from coming around, so I took it from them. It's cute, isn't it?"

"It is! It should work, Bunny!"

"I made the little golden girdle for it." Bunny smiled as she indicated the doll's tiny belt of glittering, gold embroidery thread around its hips. "It didn't look complete without it."

Honey reached for the spell pouch hanging on her belt. "All right. Put little Fairer Than on the table between us and I'll read Sugar's words of reversal."

Bunny took the chair opposite while Honey opened the pouch and carefully poured the remaining enchanted sugar on the sitting doll's head. The sugar formed a pyramid. Honey turned the pouch inside out, revealing the words written on the fabric. She glanced at Bunny.

"Do you want to do the spell?" Honey offered the pouch.

Bunny looked at her in surprise. "But I didn't hear Sugar explain it. You can do it, Honey! It should be you, since you cast it."

Honey sighed, laying the pouch down. She took Bunny's hands from across the table. The doll lay between their outstretched arms.

"Okay. Here goes."

She read what was written on the fabric.

"By these words, the two who were met, polar opposites, let the spell be unsaid. Take these complements and reverse again!"

Honey nodded to Bunny.

"Reverse again," they said in unison.

A gust of wind suddenly swept through the open windows. It hit Honey's back and blew the sugar atop the doll's head into Bunny's face.

Bunny sneezed, then coughed. Honey watched, horrified, as Bunny let go and wiped her eyes of twinkling, fading sugar dust.

When Bunny could look at Honey again, they stared.

"What just happened?" Honey said.

Bunny shuddered. She gripped her chair's armrests.

Then, Bunny was no longer Bunny.

❧

Bunny took a breath that felt like fire. Her chest felt bigger, heavier. She saw blue sky and trees along the shoreline. Water lapped around her body.

She was sitting in The Lady's Lake, soaked through.

♦

Dean flailed. Her boot scraped on metal. She steadied herself and searched the dim light. She was in the cage that sat in Pop's dungeon.

"Hey!" She shook the bars. "*Heyyyy!*"

She was cold and still inside, and the sunlight through the dungeon's lone window looked paltry and thin. Hunger gnawed. She buried her head against her arms.

"Aw, *hell*," she cried.

The door above opened and her father call down.

"Yu Ying? Is that you?"

"Yeah." She sniffed. "Somehow…I lost my body, was in someone else's, but now I'm back. Why am I in this cell?"

Shang Yu cackled. His henchmen carried him down.

"Welcome home, first daughter!" he hailed when the henchmen let him down before the cage. "How glad we are that you know nothing. Now come, come-come, we ride out to inspect our forces!"

"Damn it!" Dean said angrily.

"*Yu Ying*," Shang Yu snarled, his eyes fiery coals. Dean stiffened, taken aback.

"When you gonna take anything serious, huh?" Shang Yu bit out. "We facing war, Yu Ying. *War*. You want to play with your cars? Go dancing? Kiss girls, when it *our* responsibility to fight the Huns? You want them to come into Enchanting Forest and Little Salem and destroy everything?"

Shang Yu threw his hand out, pointing imperiously away.
"Okay then, *go!*"

Dean breathed, though she didn't need to. She remembered how Fairer Than's hot blood sang, how the trees
spoke, how small creatures and hidden faerie lived, feeling
no threat of death from her. She remembered the hurt she'd
put on the water maiden's face because Dean had—

Dean had acted like a vampire.

"You're right, Pop," she said, her voice rough. "There's so
much to protect."

She took hold of the bars and shook them.

"Let's go!" she shouted.

CHAPTER FIVE
Not Bunny

Fairer Than stared into Honey's eyes, acutely aware that she was in Bunny's house, that her body felt smaller, and that she had a heart that was beating very fast.

If I am one of the crones...I shall nap for the rest of the day.

"Hi," Honey said, staring back. "Who are you?"

"I'm," Fairer Than said and abruptly stopped. She put a hand to her mouth.

"I'm Bunny," she whispered behind her hand, marveling at the sound of Bunny's voice issuing from her lips.

"No, you're not," Honey said.

"I am Fairer Than," Fairer Than said more firmly, dropping her hand. "We must get Bunny back."

"Boy." Honey slumped in her seat, then picked up a red-haired doll sitting on the table.

"Is that myself?" Fairer Than said with surprise.

"Thanks to our spell, Bunny must be you now," Honey mused. "Unless she's in the doll."

"Why would she be in the doll? That would leave my

body dead." Fairer Than took the doll. It looked very much like her, right down to the figure.

"By my power, speak, little doll," she commanded. "Tell us who you are."

Energy, electric and warm, rose within and enveloped her hand and the doll.

This is Bunny's power, not mine.

"I am a doll," the doll said in a tiny voice.

Fairer Than looked at Honey.

"I didn't say anything," Honey said. "And you're right, if you're here, Bunny has to be in your body. Or, Dean's body! And Dean would then still be in your body. Do you know where your body is?" she added.

"I don't know where that wretched vampire has my body," Fairer Than said patiently. "I do know that when I was the vampire, her father imprisoned me in their compound. The vampire's body should be in that prison, still."

Fairer Than rose. She hid the doll high in a display cabinet behind a large Delft platter of Dutch windmills, where she hoped Bunny's smaller aunts couldn't reach. When she returned to her seat, she remembered to smooth out her pencil skirt behind her as she had seen girls dressed like Bunny do. She tried to adjust the garters of her stockings through the fabric of her skirt. Then she reached into her blouse and picked at her bra strap. It occurred to her that she'd more experience at removing such garments from women than familiarity with how to wear them.

I think I may be wearing one of their modern foundation garments. An elastic girdle.

She recalled her own golden girdle and hoped that if Bunny were in her body she didn't hurt herself on the sharpened dragon scale that dangled from the belt's end.

"Okay," Honey said. She held fingers up, as if to denote her thinking process. Fairer Than waited patiently while Honey gathered her thoughts.

"You stay here," Honey said. "Bunny is either you, or Dean. You said Dean was locked up at her family's house. If Bunny's there, then I should go there. If Dean is there, then she knows where your body is. If Dean is still you, she should come back here. I can't think where else she'd want to go."

"Oh I don't know, back to hell?" Fairer Than suggested.

"Hey." Honey pointed at her. "Be nice. It's weird seeing Bunny look so snotty."

Fairer Than looked down, contrite.

"Bunny is a good girl," Fairer Than said. She studied her hands, which were soft and small. But she could feel the strength in the wrists, palms, and fingers, no doubt from kneading dough.

"That's right," Honey said. "Now what was I saying?"

"You said that if the vampire were in my body she would still return here."

"And if Bunny were in your body, she would return here too," Honey said. "Unless she's in a prison." She looked pleased with herself for having figured out all possible outcomes. She straightened.

"You stay here. I'll go to Dean's house. Even if it is full of old vampires."

"Do you know where it is?"

Honey looked at her determinedly.

"I'll go outside and keep a lookout," she then declared.

"Very well." Fairer Than leaned back and threw an arm behind her chair.

"Don't sit like that, it isn't proper!" Honey smacked

Fairer Than on the knee. "Can you try to be nice and not make Bunny look like such a bad girl?"

"I'll try." Fairer Than immediately sat up, knees together and her hands resting on them.

Honey went to the front door, muttering about bad faeries. She grabbed a ball of string from a sewing basket. Once Honey exited, only the steady tick tock of the cuckoo clock sounded.

"Proper," Fairer Than repeated.

The oak console by the front door bore a mirror with a carved frame of painted flowers and hooks holding drawstring bags, knitted scarves, tied children's mittens, and a large ring with keys.

Children's mittens. Bunny would have been the only child in the house.

Fairer Than rose to inspect them. Bunny's face appeared in the mirror.

Fairer Than covered her mouth, stifling a sound suddenly joyful and then sad.

"I," she said softly to her own reflection, "I do miss you."

The heart in her chest beat, thunderous and fast. She thought the organ half-expanded with bursting happiness and half-crushed by the overwhelming compression of poignancy. Bunny's eyes shone with joy yet her mouth crept into a half-smile that seemed rueful.

"It is good to see you," Fairer Than whispered, and she wondered why it hurt to speak.

Energy rose within Bunny's body in response to her heightened emotions, the power vibrant and electric. She tamped it down.

That's her magic.

She visualized wrapping the bright energy carefully like

one would a baby in swaddling clothes. She lulled it to sleep, and therefore away from her ability to call upon it. A witch's power was a very different power, and Fairer Than was a magical being. She did not know what it was like to muster power rather than just *be* it. Magic summoned was best left alone, in her estimation, and recalled what her wife of long ago had been capable of.

Bunny's aunts chattered on the walk.

"Then we chased the faerie out!" Weirdette gleefully exclaimed. "With a horseshoe, we did!"

"Well, fer trespassing, ye could've made her wash our floors first," Aunt Agoosta remarked. Agoosta was a hefty woman, tall, big of bosom, and generously pear-shaped. She sighed often when speaking, as if life were a heavy matter. Fairer Than believed that Agoosta was the youngest of the three aunts living with Bunny, for she seemed to do, with Bunny's help, nearly all the household upkeep while Hauntette and Weirdette napped or went on adventures.

The door opened and Agoosta entered first.

"*Och*! That cousin of yers! Honey isn't merely visiting, is she, Bunny? Never mind. I don't know what she's doing with that ball of string, but as long as she doesn't tangle 'erself and the forest with her. Eh heh-heh-heh!" Agoosta chuckled. She carried a twenty-pound flour sack. "Bunny, help me with the flour."

"Of course, Aunt Agoosta," Fairer Than smoothly said, and took the sack. The weight of it immediately brought her arms down.

As she struggled to handle the bag with more leverage, placing it on her hip like she would carrying a child, she saw Agoosta gaze at her strangely. Aunt Weirdie peered behind Agoosta's arm, her eyes wide.

I am a horrible actress, Fairer Than thought.

"Dear Baker women," she attempted.

"Who are ye?" Weirdette shrieked. "Bind 'er! *Bind 'er!*"

Fairer Than tossed the sack back at Aunt Agoosta, who caught it, exclaiming, "oh my!" while Fairer Than fled for the kitchen and out the scullery door. She slammed it and hurried through the back garden and its gate.

Once through, she ran for the nearest tall tree and leapt for a sturdy branch. She missed.

With great effort she leapt again, caught hold, and used her feet to push up from the tree trunk.

"Careful! Careful!" Fairer Than admonished as she struggled to hook a leg over the branch. Her arms burned with the effort. "This body has a different strength!"

With great effort, she hoisted herself up, already regretting the scraping she'd given palms and fingers unused to tree climbing. Just as she hid herself behind the thick, leafy branches, Weirdette ran through the back gate, brandishing a lasso. She passed beneath Fairer Than's tree and disappeared down the path.

"Oi! Weirdette! Oi've the net!" Hauntette shouted, waving a hooped fishing net on a stick. She ran after Weirdette.

"*Bunny!*" Weirdette shrieked in the distance. "Or whoever you are! *You come back with our Bunny!*"

Once Hauntette disappeared over the ridge, Fairer Than carefully dropped to the ground. She adjusted her undergarments, straightened her skirt and blouse, and then quickly made her way around the cottage.

"For such little old ladies, I do admire their tenacity," she said. "They love Bunny so."

She felt a lump suddenly form in her throat. She tried to swallow past it.

"The heart of this body is loving, indeed," she gruffly said.

♦

At the front gate of the Baker cottage, Honey rolled out a ball of string she'd tied to a nail. She believed that the ball could last her a hundred feet. Then she would tie on another ball of string and keep going while still safely able to return back to Bunny's house.

No, wait. She didn't have a second ball of string.

Fairer Than walked from the back of the cottage towards her.

Honey couldn't doubt that it was *her*, no matter what form the faerie might have. Fairer Than strolled with hips that sensually defined both gait and pace. She held her shoulders like she could take on Atlas's burden, easily. And the way she gazed, with heavy lids that hid smoky thoughts—such a look was disconcerting enough that Honey had to drop her own regard, like so many probably did, to Fairer Than's mouth.

And she couldn't say that Fairer Than sneered. It was more like her lips ever so slightly...pouted.

There really is no way for her to act nice, she's just bad, Honey thought. *But boy, does she make a person want to kiss her.*

Realizing she was thinking of Bunny's mouth in that way, Honey put her hands on her hips.

"You couldn't stay put?" she demanded as Fairer Than approached.

"Your aunts chased me out," Fairer Than said. "Let us leave before they try to bind me. I will help you look for Bunny. Or for my body. Do we need to bring your string?"

Honey wound the string back up and left the ball on the garden wall.

"I just had a thought. We could scry for her," Honey suggested as they left the Baker cottage. "Although her body is already here...I wonder how that spell would work?"

"If scrying did follow Bunny's essence and she were in the vampire compound, the casting would not penetrate their walls," Fairer Than said. "They've signs drawn to deter spying."

"Really?" Honey said thoughtfully. "So it's already started. Or the vampires had always been that way. Y'know...I never liked royal courts. Vampire families are like that, I bet. Full of spies and intrigue."

Fairer Than looked at Honey in surprise. "I cannot speak for the ways of vampires, but royal courts are."

"And if they're not spying, they make stuff up. Do you know those guys?" Honey pointed ahead. Two faerie men stood alongside the path, their rich garb torn. One had a floppy, velvet cap with a broken feather. The other sported a bruise on his chin. In the latter's hand was a two-prong dowsing stick with a strand of red hair tied to its end. The stick bent and quivered towards Fairer Than.

The men smirked. Fairer Than halted and blocked Honey with her arm.

"Honey, return to the cottage," Fairer Than ordered.

Honey whipped out her wand. Before she could enact a protection spell, a cloud of tiny faeries descended.

The winged creatures swarmed Honey, screaming, stinging her with pins and pulling her down by her hair and clothes. Her blouse tore. She waved frantically to ward them off, tripped backwards, and fell. Once she was down, they struck her with their tiny fists and gave her kicks for good measure. Honey curled up and stayed that way until the gleeful laughter of the faeries and the beating of their wings faded away.

Honey slowly brought her arms down. She was alone. The little faeries had tossed her hat high in a tree.

"Ow," Honey said miserably.

Getting beat up, whether by windup dolls or vampire rabbits, really did a number on a girl. Though Honey had her fair share of fights, it was still hard to pick herself up and dust off after losing. Honey felt liked she'd fled through stinging nettles again—without being pursued by a sorceress queen's fire-breathing dogs. She made her limping way back to the cottage.

At the gate, Aunt Hauntie and Weirdie stood with net and lasso, defending the garden against a thoroughly soaked Fairer Than. The front gate was broken off its hinges. Fairer Than held her hands up.

"I'm so confused," Honey said.

Honey limped up and assured the aunties that Fairer Than was not herself but—once Honey affirmed—Bunny. The aunties saw it was true and urged Bunny inside. Bunny approached the front door first and tore it off its hinges.

"*Oh dear,*" she cried.

The sound of the door being ripped out of its frame brought Aunt Agoosta running from the kitchen, her rolling pin held up. But after assurances that Fairer Than was really Bunny, they ushered Bunny to a chair. Agoosta fetched towels and Weirdette and Hauntette brought stools to sit close and stare. Honey flopped into the chair before Bunny, looked at her bewildered cousin, and sighed.

When Agoosta returned, she dropped a towel around Bunny's shoulders and was about to rub her hair dry when she peered down at her.

"You've dried so quickly!" Agoosta said.

"I'm really warm," Bunny said as Agoosta rubbed her hair. "Honey, you look terrible. And your hat!"

"I got beat up. And tiny faerie feet stomped on my hat. So, Bunny—since you're Fairer Than, then Dean's Dean, and Fairer Than's you."

"Is Fairer Than here?"

Honey shook her head. "These faerie guys nabbed her."

"Wipe yer feet now, dearie," Agoosta bade, giving Bunny another towel. She turned for the kitchen. "Honey, do ye want the first aid kit?" she called.

"No thanks, Aunt Agoosta! Wearing a million band aids would look silly."

Honey watched as Bunny moved carefully and slowly to wipe her feet.

"Those are big feet," Honey remarked.

"Oooo, lookit the ring," Weirdette said, as Bunny bent over. Weirdette pointed at the gold ring used to tie Fairer Than's hair back.

"Aye, that's a *ruler's* ring." Hauntette peered at the jewelry with her spyglass. "Used as a bauble for 'er tresses!

Harumph!"

"Oooo, and lookit the armlet." Weirdette pointed.

"Aye, that's power too," Hauntette said, inspecting its glyphs.

"Ooooo," Weirdette simply said when Bunny straightened. Weirdette pointed at the golden girdle hanging heavily around Bunny's hips.

"'Tis a most powerful girdle, that." Hauntette studied the markings on the gold medallions. "A warrior queen's girdle."

Weirdette reached over and poked one of the large fangs hanging alongside the medallions. Agoosta returned bearing a steaming cup of tea.

"Dragon's teeth," Agoosta sighed when she looked down at what everyone peered at. She gave the cup to Bunny, who held it gingerly.

"You mean from some old relative," Honey said. "Family mementos."

The aunts looked at her.

"Oh, okay," Honey said. "Nice trophies."

The teacup shattered in Bunny's hand, splattering hot tea.

"Oh dear!" Bunny exclaimed. Agoosta tutted and left to fetch another cloth. Honey jumped up for the house broom.

While Honey swept up the last of the china fragments and Agoosta mopped Bunny's chest, Weirdette inspected the medallions of the girdle's dangling end. Fairer Than's belt end fell in such a way that one had to look at her crotch, therefore Honey had never taken the opportunity to study the intriguing ornament that terminated the belt.

Weirdette poked at the object, an iridescent shard encased in engraved gold. Large enough to be a squat blade, three fingers wide, it looked nearly like opaque glass, but as Honey peered closer she could see it was organic—a single scale from the skin of some large beast: a dragon's.

"Careful! You could take yer fingers off with that," Agoosta cautioned.

"Ooo, just a closer look!" Weirdette worked her bony fingers beneath to lift the object from Bunny's lap.

"*Oh*," Weirdette exclaimed when the scale's weight trapped her fingers. She tugged.

"How about we—" Honey tried to lift the dragon scale by its encasement and found she couldn't. "Look at—Fairer Than's—stuff later. Me and Bunny have important—Goddess, this is heavy!"

Bunny picked up the belt end Honey struggled with and moved it away. Aunt Weirdie snatched her fingers back.

"All the medallions be serpent's gold, smelt in the heart of the Earth," Hauntette said darkly.

"Or on Jupiter," Honey said. "You'd think it had its own gravitational pasture."

"Field," Bunny said.

"What?" Honey couldn't recall if that was how Sugar would say it. "Okay, everybody! Show and tell later. Bunny and I have a body to retrieve."

Weirdette and Hauntette withdrew, grumbling, and departed for the sitting room. Agoosta returned to the kitchen.

"When ye're back in your own body, Bunny, help me with the cheese moulds," Agoosta called.

"Yes, Aunt Agoosta!" Bunny said.

"Are you making brie? I love brie." Honey rose. "Okay, let's go."

"Not yet." Bunny's tone was contrite. "I'm a volcano inside. I could start breathing fire at any moment. And I can't seem to stop breaking things."

"Bunny, we have to get your body."

"I think Fairer Than will take good care of it," Bunny said reassuringly.

"I don't know." Honey sat down again and put her head in her hands. "I mean, no, you're right, she *will* take care of you. But...I guess it's getting to me. Or maybe I shouldn't have had those fish tacos. I've lost Fairer Than twice today, and this time in your body, which isn't exactly a dragon's body or a vampire's body. It can get hurt. And Fairer Than being in it is like putting a tiger inside a rabbit. I don't think those faerie guys are going to be nice."

"Oh," Bunny said, realization dawning. "Okay. Just...give me a minute."

Bunny closed her eyes, apparently to meditate.

"So, you feel her dragon's power," Honey said, curious. "But what's her faerie nature like?"

Bunny opened her eyes and frowned. "I'm not sure. I don't feel very...aloof."

"I can tell it's you in there. You don't have that look faeries usually have. Like you're beyond our ken. Faraway and kind of perfect. The lack of feelings make them like that. They don't have hearts like us."

"They don't. But Fairer Than is part human and dragon, so she does have a heart like us. I think."

"Let me listen." Honey took off her hat, moved her hair back, and pressed an ear to Bunny's chest. "You're hot, you'd think something was keeping all that blood pumping. I hear an echo."

When Honey lifted her head, Bunny touched where her heart would be.

"I've heard that dragons hide their hearts," Bunny said, thoughtful.

"You've the ghost of it in your chest, that's for sure. Ready now?"

Bunny smiled, incredulous. Fairer Than's generous lips curled and her green eyes widened. If there was any doubt as to Fairer Than's true age, Honey could see the difference right then. A young and innocent soul looked at her from Fairer Than's eyes.

"The longer you try to be 'you' in Fairer Than's body, the less 'dragon' I bet you'll become," Honey explained. "I don't mean to push, but faeries can do some mean business. Your body might be a toadstool by now, or a spider, or Mab's left slipper. If you think you can play the part, you should walk in on their turf like a dragon right away and get your body back."

Bunny nodded. She slowly rose.

The chair's arm snapped off in her hand.

"Wow." Honey took the broken armrest. "Save that for the faeries."

♦

Bunny walked carefully through the door and garden gate she broke, noticing the pillywiggins peeping from the flowers. They giggled at her progress. If she bumped Honey, she might send her cousin tumbling. How did lions gently handle lambs? She'd asked Dean once how she managed her preternatural strength.

"By being very careful with witch girls," Dean had answered, grinning.

But Dean's true answer was that she summoned it. The power was there to leap far or lift a small car, but it slept until called upon. Dean didn't have to worry about breaking pencils and squeezing Bunny too hard in an embrace.

Fairer Than, however, *was* power. Bunny felt it course right into her fingertips and toes. Her body was dense like a stone. Bunny recalled how Fairer Than held herself. She'd never suspected from their first meeting that Fairer Than had been anything more than some beautiful faerie. Yet Bunny was experiencing right then what it was like to be a being who could easily toss her human self to the moon.

Then a thought occurred that—had she less Fairer Than's iron gut and more her own soft belly—might inspire a sickening drop: Fairer Than could have easily killed Dean any time during the challenge fight of Sweetheart's Night.

"Now those guys, the way they were dressed, they were high faeries, so they must be from the Court," Honey said as they walked. Goblins stared balefully from the underbrush. A tiny gnome wheeled his barrow around a tree root and tipped his hat to Bunny.

"How awful for her to be without her strength," Bunny said worriedly.

"She could try calling on your power, but she probably won't. If I were in your body, I wouldn't," Honey declared.

Bunny briefly laughed. "Are you talking about what happened on Sweetheart's Night? That wasn't me, Honey. It was *dragon's* breath. Given to me by Fairer Than."

"Sure it was." Honey said. She looked around. "Okay, here's the hard part: finding the Faerie Court."

"Oh, I sometimes know where it is."

"Not that hard, then. How do you know?"

"Um." Bunny felt sheepish. "Since dealing with Fairer Than, I'd made it my business to know. Just in case...well, just in case. I'd ask the forest's stones, and they'd point the way. The Court moves around a lot."

Honey looked at her expectantly.

"I'm not going to try casting in this body," Bunny said. "I could blow up a mountain. But I do have faerie senses now. That should make things easier."

"I bet you can blow up a little hill right now. Mom told us how you summoned a triple portal into Hecate's realm. To save Dean's life, right? Sugar did the math, called it a mage-level invocation. She was impressed."

"I only got lucky that it worked," Bunny exclaimed. "Sugar is a *magus*, she could do that summoning asleep. I'm nowhere as—" She halted at Honey's expression. Bunny had seen that look passed between her aunties.

Honey took hold of Bunny's arms.

"I know it's so soon," Honey said. "Like me getting lost when I was four. Like Sugar leaving for the bigger world."

Bunny shook her head. Why was she the only skeptic? She still felt like a pie-maker with no great mage hidden inside. She looked to the sky and closed her eyes rather than try to extricate herself from Honey's touch.

"I'm sorry," Honey said.

The two faerie men bore Fairer Than away, then drew her through the veil of enchantment surrounding a forest hollow. They pushed her to sit on a fallen tree trunk. A tiny insect band played. Little faeries industriously dealt with the broken remnants of a party seemingly gone awry, though a few disheveled Daughters of the Court stood nearby. None danced to the sprightly music, which somehow sounded forced, mustering gaiety.

Fairer Than studied the Daughters, wondering why they appeared fearful. They whispered behind their hands, but some words reached her human ears.

"Is it starting? Strife and darkness?" one whispered. "Those two, in *one* form!"

"*She*, who ignited, and nearly burned our forest down," another said softly.

"And *she*, infatuated, who loves the sword and war horn," a third murmured.

Fairer Than's lips twisted.

This prattle.

"How The Fairest has fallen," one of the men suddenly mocked. "Hardly better than thy *betters*, if ever. When we speak before our queen, we shall see how thou *fares*."

His companion touched his arm to forestall more remarks. The two walked off, as if to impress that with their task done they'd no concern for her, whatsoever. But though they feigned such attitude, Fairer Than was certain they wanted to gloat more. The two were new to her—perhaps why they'd received the task of fetching her. No faerie that knew her would have dared.

That they wisely ceased engagement meant they'd become aware of their sister faeries' wary behavior. The males sought conversation with the Daughters of the Court, only to be shunned.

Fairer Than was only slightly amused. She could not be certain what had wrecked the party, shaken the Daughters, and bruised the men's faces, but since the vampire was the last known inhabitant of her body, Fairer Than could guess.

Regardless, she wouldn't mind engaging the two toadies later—once she was back in her more formidable form.

For now, I will do nothing to endanger Bunny's body.

The phoukas, pixies, and hobgoblins, however, had other intentions. They gathered around, tugged at her skirt, clawed her stockings, clamored into her lap to pull up her blouse, or fluttered about in the air, yanking on her hair. They made faces, jeered, and taunted. When they pinched her, Fairer Than raised a hand, then lowered it. Any moment, they might take advantage of her present state as a susceptible mortal. But Fairer Than kept her gaze on each little face.

Bewitch me, beguile me, or bewilder me; I know thy every trick. Try, and thou shalt never perceive when I, Fairer Than, will render you all—

"Crisps," she murmured, her lip lifting to reveal teeth.

The little ones fled.

A chubby child wearing a tilted, jeweled crown then danced into the clearing, twirling in her oversized gown tied up with ribbons. She fluttered her tissue paper wings. Voices hushed and music stilled. Reaching into her gold pot, the child strewed her path with sparkling cobwebs, pollen dust, and motes. When she raised her star-tipped wooden wand, Fairer Than obligingly bent to be tapped on the head. She touched the little girl's rosy cheek and looked into her peaceful eyes. The babe would remember little when returned to her crib and mother. The little girl twirled away and disappeared at the clearing's end, trailing fading sparkles.

Titania stepped into the hollow.

Bunny ran through the woods with Honey cradled in her arms.

It seemed faster to carry her cousin than have Honey try to keep up with her. Bunny was listening to every part of the forest—an endless turning of the radio dial to find the right broadcast that would lead her to the Court, and often she was wrong about what signal to follow.

Bunny's new body held a sensory depth and magical acuity that nearly overwhelmed. The Enchanting Forest, her longtime home, lived and breathed, right down to the twigs. Its presence pulsed. The tree trunks changed as spriggans emerged to stare and then melted back into their trees. The wind whispered songs. Bunny listened, fascinated.

"Bunny," Honey said as she waved a hand before Bunny's face. "Have you dialed to the correct faerie channel yet?"

Chastised, Bunny focused. A silent invitation drew her to a faerie ring. But the mushroom circle and the tiny faeries dancing around it did not harbor the two males Honey had described. Bunny ran closer to the lake.

"I think..." Bunny listened. The faint noise of a more festive gathering was near.

However, the sound of it seemed tense rather than gay.

"Do you hear that music?" she asked.

"I hear nothing but trees rustling," Honey said.

Bunny placed Honey on her feet. Honey adjusted her skirt.

"This might be the one." Bunny straightened. "You stay back and I'll go in."

"After the butt-kicking I got, I'm okay with that. But I'll rush in the moment something's wrong. Do you know what you're going to do?"

"Yes."

Honey looked at her expectantly. Bunny simply winked, well aware that faeries were listening.

"Goddess," Honey said, breathless. "Don't *do* that. It's bad enough that you're in that body, so I shouldn't even think it. But if I wanted to sleep with a girl I probably could fall for

Fairer Than. For a night, anyway."

"Oh," Bunny said, flustered. "Sorry."

"I'm never going to forget how she smells." Honey leaned in and breathed deeply. "There. I finally get to do it without her smirking at me. How did you resist her?"

"I barely did," Bunny admitted. "I'd wanted her. Badly. Then I realized…she wasn't what I needed."

The music stopped. Bunny stilled, and the forest did as well, as if holding its breath.

"Something…" Bunny said, hushed.

"What?" Honey whispered.

Within the forest's heart, something or someone spoke. But Bunny heard no sounds, only felt the intention. It was like a scolding delivered via poured ice water.

"Someone important is angry," Bunny softly said.

A wreath of lights shone on Titania's brow. No other faeries accompanied her and no smile was present on her face. The faeries stilled.

Before any could bow or curtsey, she raised a hand.

All present folded upon themselves and fled into shadows and inside invisible places. The hollow emptied.

Fairer Than did not kneel or rise. Even in Bunny's body, she stood taller than her queen.

Titania touched Fairer Than upon the forehead.

"By this touch art thou impeded," she said.

The magic within Fairer Than disappeared from her awareness, a curtain of night pulled down.

Is Bunny such a threat?

Titania looked down coldly.

"Thou art a disgrace to faerie, and to us."

"In what manner, my Queen?" Fairer Than asked politely. "I am a mongrel. How can I not be less than the perfection thou art?"

"Thou were accepted as ours," Titania said.

"Aye, half thine."

"And thou fixates, beyond reason, with one of *them*."

Fairer Than schooled her surprise. Titania had no quarrel with witches.

"Thou hast myself," Fairer Than admitted.

An uneasy silence fell.

"Dear Queen, thou recalls my good wife?" Fairer Than then said. "For such graciousness as she had possessed doth reflect in—"

Titania's gaze iced. "Speak not of Brienne. *This* one consorts with those who walk again."

Vampires.

Fairer Than stared at Titania, pieces falling into place.

As Queen, there were many things Titania could not directly address without prematurely alerting her gossiping subjects. If she knew of the vampire plot brewing in the Steppes, she would not speak of it—and of what it would do to the Enchanting Forest and the towns, draining those within it.

Bunny is no threat. She would not help her beau in that way, Fairer Than wanted to say, but she suspected—

Her Queen had a deeper fear. Fairer Than could not promise that *she* would not aid Bunny.

And should you lead our kin deeper into the forest, away from strife, harm may still follow through one like myself. For I haven't the good sense to let Bunny go.

Fairer Than shut her eyes briefly, not wanting Titania to

see. A solution had come to her, one reckless.

"I am guilty," Fairer Than answered in a careless tone. "Of such foolery. But if that part, *thy* part, of myself were excised, perhaps what muddles me so would also go. I'd know myself better."

Titania gazed, incredulous. "Thou believes such a thing?"

"I might finally understand *love*, for one thing," Fairer Than snapped.

"Do not assume that love itself is thy problem."

"All that I've done and have *suffered* from have been for that reason!"

"Blame not love." Titania's tone was ice. "But rejection. For thou art *flawed*."

Fairer Than's eyes stung. Tears sprang. To her surprise, a sob escaped, her chest filled with pangs.

The visits to Bunny's window, the rejections, the drunkenness, and the girls who could not help her forget—

Fairer Than clutched her aching chest and knew then that she'd never been a young girl, for a girl's heart was so vulnerable.

Bunny had not wanted her, and it hurt so.

Titania's curious gaze was cool and distant; the eyes of a creature beyond ken. Was that what Bunny saw in Fairer Than?

Her tears ceased.

"I am *muddled*, dear Queen," Fairer Than corrected, steeling her voice. "By the warring aspects of my nature. If it be a flaw, I can no more mend it than a stink bug claim it will no longer stink. I implore you, great and wise Titania, accept it."

"Thou would persist? Thou art a poor human mimic.

Namely, an idiot."

"How may I cease to be so? Thou chose to give it thy attention. Thou should mend myself."

"Thrice an idiot."

"*Mend* me," Fairer Than snarled.

Titania's eyes lightened. Understanding dwelled, as if she knew exactly what Fairer Than intended.

Kiss me not and bid me no farewell, sweet Titania and Brienne's godmother.

Titania raised her hand. Her voice was as smooth as water, gently pouring.

"That which is ours to take, we take."

Fairer Than heard great bells. She disappeared like swiftly fading sunlight.

◆

Bunny felt herself disappear again.

"*Bunny*?" Honey cried from afar.

Bunny became aware of herself—her true self, body and all—sitting in a sun-dappled clearing. Her breaths came short. She rose with a start.

Distant bells faintly tinkled, then dwindled with the breeze. She saw no one, but she was certain faerie eyes watched.

She jumped over mushrooms and ran. As she burst out of the clearing, a chorus of faraway laughter echoed.

◆

"Bunny?" Honey cried, reaching.

But Bunny faded in her grasp until nothing could be felt

or seen. Honey groped the air in case Bunny had turned invisible.

"Oh boy," she said, dropping her arms. She had a sinking feeling that Bunny's disappearance — of her *and* Fairer Than's body — wasn't a continuance of Sugar's original spell.

She spun around, seeing nothing but evening light and trees. The Court itself could be present for all she knew, with invisible beings pointing and laughing. She picked up a long stick.

After thrashing the foliage, shouting halloos that left her hoarse, and finding not one faerie, Honey dropped her stick, head bowed.

"I'm sorry, Bunny."

She looked up. The sun dipped. Night would soon arrive, and Honey could not remain. She took a deep breath.

"Once more into the world. If I try hard to get to Little Salem's soda shop, maybe I'll end up back at Bunny's."

She walked resolutely into the darkening forest.

Fairer Than fell. Mud met her face and she impacted with a *sploosh* that sent mud flying.

She pulled herself up from the sucking mess. She was in Goodie Gertie's pigpen — once more in her own body — and she burned, hotter than the sun.

Her dragon's vision viewed the spotted pig before her as a pulsing, yellow beacon.

Smoke curled from Fairer Than's nostrils and mouth.

The pig squealed.

CHAPTER SIX
My Heart

Fairer Than marched from Goodie Gertie's small farm for the lake, her body covered in mud and smoldering of fire. Birds and small creatures fled, bright, hot orange bodies to her dragon's vision. The cool, blue shape of a lizard scurried quickly out of sight. Fairer Than drew in her flames before traversing the forest. Smoke rose from her nostrils as hardened mud cracked and fell crumbling.

"'Muddled?' Aye, she *showed* me muddled," Fairer Than growled.

When she reached the lake, she was not surprised that a rowboat sat moored not far from the faerie hollow.

Perhaps her once-queen had anticipated what Fairer Than would do next. More likely, she hadn't had a clue, and the boat's presence was pure serendipity. Whatever the case, Fairer Than expelled a fiery breath to calm the dragon within. Her dragon-vision dimmed and instead of cool, blue shapes, she saw a mere wooden boat and sunlit waters lapping. She took hold of the rope lassoed to a rock, and cast off.

What need had she for a boat? If she sprouted leathery wings and grew her scaly tail, she could fly for her destination. But she suspected that once transformed, she would not stop but only fly on forever, as cold and remote in eye as her once-queen.

"What did I just do?" Fairer Than asked the boat.

She'd made a decision while in a girl's *human* body—a decision made with a loving *heart*—

Titania had shown Fairer Than what she'd thought of that, by dropping her in mud.

With her faerie nature gone like a dandelion plucked and blown, she felt like a beast, untempered. She needed her heart. She could ask Lady to retrieve it, but to have her once-kin witness her in her present state—was there any need to discuss it?

"I'd asked for it, didn't I?" Fairer Than pushed the boat into the water. She jumped in and seated herself. "'Get rid of me,' I'd demanded!"

"Honey?" she heard someone call in the woods. Fairer Than paused, automatically receptive to the endearment.

"Fairer Than!" Bunny hurried from the woods.

Fairer Than watched how Bunny ran, tucking her blouse back into her skirt's waistband. Bunny's body did not move like the vampire's but like a woman's; like Bunny.

"Alas," Fairer Than said bitterly.

She hunched in the boat and willed herself invisible, though she hadn't that power.

"We must talk," Bunny called from the shore. "Please come back, Fairer Than."

Fairer Than looked at the sky.

"If we must," she sighed.

She turned around in her seat, took hold of the oars, and with one pull, drove the boat to shore.

Once she'd helped Bunny into the boat, Fairer Than sat down and resumed rowing. Each powerful stroke sent them knifing across the lake. She ignored Bunny's gaze.

"It is you. But...you're different," Bunny said.

"Mud is a new look for me."

"Besides that. You've changed. What happened with the faeries? Are you all right?"

"I should ask you that," Fairer Than said. She finally looked at Bunny, who appeared unhurt. "Did any harm you after you were returned to your body?"

Bunny shook her head. "I was alone. Now tell me what happened to you."

Fairer Than laughed.

"Refinement," she said. "That is all. I wonder how I look to you now, without that aspect which first charmed you. I only learned later that you were enamored of faerie kind."

"What?" Bunny whispered.

Fairer Than fell silent and rowed. Smoke curled from a corner of her mouth and realization dawned on Bunny's face. And fear.

She turned and blew smoke to the side.

"Fairer Than," Bunny whispered and reached for her.

Fairer Than moved her knee away from Bunny's touch.

"Bunny, you've a remarkable heart," Fairer Than said. "When I was in your body I desired to be things I could only describe as being you. Warm, loving...giving. Such aspects are not well known to me. If I miss them, then I miss you."

Bunny's head briefly moved; a gesture of bafflement.

"Fairer Than...I would think such feelings came from you, no matter the body you're in. Is it the organ that rules us, or is it really that we rule the organ?"

"For as long as I've lived, I don't know that answer," Fairer Than said miserably. "Perhaps I demanded the wrong gift of Titania. She should have taken the human part, and as a whole faerie, would I never know this pain."

Bunny stared in dismay. "Fairer Th—"

"Why do I desire an aspect—*once more*, and one I'd made myself forget, that I was never suited for?" Fairer Than interrupted. "I had blamed having been a man for my last failure, but even as a woman I would have left you to die again. And I have you confused with another," she hastily added at Bunny's look of bewilderment.

"You've lost someone," Bunny said.

"As those who love, do. And now can recall to the most painful detail with all my faerie nature taken. Yet I still lack." Fairer Than briefly touched her chest in emphasis. "Perhaps I can't learn that which you already know in your heart, which are important things, essential things, inherent to both breath and love."

"Fairer Than," Bunny said softly. She reached again.

"Don't."

Bunny stilled.

"And say nothing," Fairer Than ordered. "I don't wish to hear it."

"Telling me to shut up will get you nowhere, Fairer Than," Bunny said hotly.

"That's more like it."

"Fairer Than, please. I know this started with Honey's spell. I wish I understood why it involved you, me, and Dean."

"Must you mention that fool," Fairer Than ground out. "And you too, for loving that dolt. She'll bring ruination."

"Wha—?" Bunny said, amazed.

"And I did like Little Salem. And liked you in it," Fairer Than muttered. Their boat entered the wide river that led out of the lake. Its waters moved quickly.

"What happened when you were in Dean's body?" Bunny demanded.

"As your cousin would say: intrigues."

"You're talking about the vampires."

"'Parasites' is a more apt term. Pretenders to an imaginary throne."

"You don't just dislike vampires, you think they're lesser, don't you?" Bunny said incredulously.

"Bunny, they are bloodsuckers," Fairer Than said. "And as for that variety of vampire that is your beau's family, they life-suck. When they can't do that, they take it from your homes, your livelihoods. How long have they tolerated living in the Twilight World, growing feebler and feebler? They waken now, and would suck this world dry if not eradicated."

"The Twilight World's peace is maintained by balance," Bunny said. "We follow the unspoken law that keeps us harmonious. The vampires can't overstep any more than the demons, fairies, or witches. You're being hateful, Fairer Than."

"I am being aware! An 'overstep' by such creatures would be the more honest action! Instead, ruin is wrought by deceit, by *fraud*. No swift stab to the back but from pins, added slowly, secretively, until you realize, finally, somewhere in your ghost heart, that thou art a pincushion, a giant, bleeding pincushion—!"

"From *love*," Fairer Than cried.

She stood. The boat rocked from her abrupt movement, carried then by a swift current. Ahead, the man-eating maelstrom appeared. The waterfall above it heralded their approach with a thunderous roar.

"And yes, I've come to hate certain vampires," she snapped.

Bunny's voice was low and raw. "You are so disrespectful of my heart."

"I am *fond* of your heart," Fairer Than said. "Not of its choices. *Why*? Why do you love that creature?"

"Because Dean, unlike her supposed 'nature,' is good! Because she tries, and just when I think maybe we shouldn't be together, she tries harder. And as a vampire, you know she doesn't have to. I can't help but love that."

The ghost-space in Fairer Than's chest twisted. A thought came to her with a barking laugh: if only she were Dean.

"Such faith you have," Fairer Than shouted. The falls above the maelstrom created a din that nearly drowned all sound.

"Isn't love 'faith,' Fairer Than?" Bunny shouted back.

"You don't know what is about to happen." Fairer Than turned and noted how swiftly they were moving towards the falls and the whirlpool beneath it. She took the rope and lassoed the jutting branch of a sunken tree stump. The boat stopped with a jerk. "I must get what I came for. We can continue arguing after, or you can agree that I am right!"

"Not about someone I love!" Bunny cried above the water's roar.

"And that is why I must jump overboard. Adieu!"

Fairer Than leapt from the boat and dove.

✦

The maelstrom pulled and Fairer Than welcomed it. She swam down and allowed it to take her, hastening her downward spiral. Her heart called, a steady beat within the whirlpool's violent motion. Fairer Than spun to the bottom and dug fingers into the rock, fighting the dragging currents that would discard her and the debris speeding by, miles away. Her heart lay beneath the stone slab she hovered above. She opened her dragon vision to the churning darkness and saw its bright, white heat through the stone.

She tore the slab up, grabbed her heart's sealed chest by the chains, and fastened it to her girdle. She pushed off from the slab and with powerful strokes, swam against the pull. She expelled fire. Just as she drove up to what her dragon vision deemed the warmer waters of the surface, she saw the fading yellow of a limp, female form rush by, carried down by the maelstrom's pull. Fairer Than turned and swam for the shape.

✦

Bunny wanted to give Fairer Than more than a piece of her mind once the faerie returned from whatever purpose had brought them to the whirlpool.

"And she better come back," Bunny griped. "She's not getting the last word!"

But her anger faded when she recalled a more somber concern. She nearly called Fairer Than 'that faerie'—that domineering, beautiful, magnificent faerie. But Fairer

Than was clearly no longer of the faerie.

Bunny's heart hurt. She tried to recall their discussion before Fairer Than had steered it into confrontation. She hadn't understood half of what Fairer Than had tried to say, or had said in that obscure manner beings of magical beginnings often communicated in. But somehow Bunny knew she was the cause for Fairer Than's loss.

She hugged herself as the boat rocked in the rushing water, her mind seeking and casting away futile solutions.

She didn't notice when wood debris swiftly approached and bumped into the taut rope mooring her boat. Trapped, the debris caused more floating wood to be caught against it.

"Wait," Bunny said, realizing the dilemma. Before she could raise her hands, the branch of the sunken tree snapped.

Bunny stared in alarm as the freed boat rocked down the churning waters for the waterfall and the whirling maelstrom beneath it. Caught in the pull, her boat soon followed the spin. Bunny motioned in the air and then tapped herself on the head.

"*Beat it, dematerialize,*" she commanded.

She did not disappear. She tried again.

"Beat it, *dematerialize!*"

The pull around the maelstrom accelerated. Bunny dove as far out as she could.

"Some—potential high witch, I am!" she sputtered when she resurfaced.

She swam hard for the sunlit shore beyond the maelstrom's spin. Evening light lent the yellow sands a warm glow. Blue shadows lay in the sandy cliffs. Arms and legs heavy, she fought the rushing current. She tried to keep her head above. The fall's thunder filled her ears, and then the maelstrom's furious roar as water inundated and sunlight disappeared.

In the darkness, she gulped water—too much water. She inhaled water. Her throat seized. She clawed as she felt herself swept around. A thousand points of pain exploded in her chest. Her limbs became stone. She sank...sank, sank, her sense of time slowing into a dreaming as she spun...

♦

Fairer Than caught the body being dragged down to the maelstrom's bottom and swam for the light. When they broke the surface she looked at whom she'd rescued.

"What?" she said, her voice shaking.

Fairer Than swam swiftly for shore.

She clambered up the sands with Bunny in her arms. Bunny was limp, her mouth slack. Her eyes were shut and she took no breath. Her body was light, too light, as if the soul had already fled. Fairer Than knew what death looked like.

"No," she said, her voice faraway.

She fell to her knees and shook Bunny.

"Awaken," she commanded.

Fairer Than's breaths came short. Puffs of flame spit from her lips. She tried to stop her fire.

"Stop it," she said fiercely. "Stop. She needs *air*."

She took a deep breath.

"Dragon's breath," she summoned.

She took Bunny by the chin and put her lips to her cold ones. She exhaled smoke. Fairer Than reared in horror.

"Gods, *lieges*," she cried. She rose with Bunny in her arms.

"O Lady of the Lake! Mab! Titania! Come to me! I would give up everything. She of the Threshold, of the Gates! Please don't take her! *Help* me!"

Fairer Than walked, seeing no one. She threw Bunny over her shoulder, as if by that act she could prove to someone, anyone: *we must go. Now.*

"Not like this," she said. "No. *No.*"

Fairer Than whimpered. Bunny was a feather, a ghost on her shoulder.

"*Help*," she wailed.

She hefted her like a babe.

Bunny convulsed. She vomited water, the ejection splattering the wet sand.

"Ah," Fairer Than cried. She thought of babies, of burping babies. She hoisted Bunny again and felt Bunny's body seize against her shoulder. Bunny retched more, water gurgling down. Fairer Than patted Bunny's back and bounced her until she heard her take her first deep breath.

"*Huuuuhh*," Bunny heaved.

Fairer Than fell to her knees and took Bunny into her arms. Bunny's stark gaze moved to Fairer Than's face, recognizing.

Bunny drew breath. Fairer Than hugged her and tears suffocated her chest. Her fire went out.

CHAPTER SEVEN
Yet

Lady rose from the maelstrom like one rising out of glass. The sister to Mab and the equal to Titania glided across the water. The Lady of the Lake looked upon Bunny and raised her hand. Titania's binding spell rose from Bunny's shivering form and dissipated.

Fairer Than stared at the spell's fading remnants. She had been so stupid.

"Thy...condition," Lady softly said.

"Not yet," Fairer Than abruptly said.

She picked up Bunny and ran away.

She ran into the woods. She ran over hill and dale. She ran Bunny back to her cottage and straight up the garden path to her front door. The aunties hurried from the kitchen and sitting room to witness her rushing through the broken door and carrying Bunny up the stairs. Fairer Than didn't know which was Bunny's chamber—she only guessed. Weirdette and Hauntette pursued.

"Not on the bed!" Weirdette screeched. "Take orf her

wet things!"

Fairer Than stared at her dumbly. She put Bunny down on the floor.

She had never fumbled so much with a woman's clothes. She helped with Bunny's blouse and skirt, leaving her shuddering in her camisole and slip. Hauntette loudly demanded answers. Fairer Than explained about Bunny's drowning as best as she could, wondering why her own voice shook.

They pushed her out of the room just as Bunny spoke.

"I'm all right," she rasped.

Fairer Than watched from the doorway while the aunties helped Bunny with her undergarments.

When Bunny was put in bed, Fairer Than retreated and sat on the steps. She had no fire inside of her.

I feel...shock? she thought in wonderment. She'd witnessed much in war and in human suffering. She'd had cause to weep a little, in the past. As much as a faerie could grieve, even for beloved Brienne. Yet right then, she believed she was experiencing that funny-looking state she'd seen in human countenances, so blank and seemingly disbelieving. It was one that had often entertained the Folk, especially when they had caused the suffering.

She felt something hanging heavily by her side and looked down. She still had her chest. She lifted it, the black seal whole. But she had no idea if the contents were still intact.

How appropriate if the egg was cracked, her heart broken.

Aunt Agoosta puffed up the stairs, carrying hot water bottles. She berated Fairer Than for pooling water and ordered her to the kitchen to take off her wet things. Fairer

Than went below, undressed, and hung her dripping garments on a drying rack by the crackling hearth. A stew pot, fragrant with cooking meat and vegetables, hung over the fire. Agoosta brought down Bunny's blouse, skirt, and undergarments and hung them on the rack. She tutted at the torn state of Bunny's stockings. Fairer Than then realized that Bunny's shoes had been lost in the maelstrom.

"Goddess, yer a big 'un," Agoosta muttered as she left again. She returned with a pile of towels and a folded bed sheet. "Wrap yerself with the sheet! And wipe orf yer mess on the stairs before we slip on them puddles!"

Fairer Than fashioned a simple toga while Agoosta prepared another kettle of hot water. Fairer Than donned her golden girdle again with the chest hanging, took the towels, then went to wipe the downstairs floorboards and stairs. She also wiped the upstairs hallway for good measure. Bunny's door stood open.

Fairer Than edged to the doorframe and peeked.

Hauntette sat in a small, wooden chair by the bed, pipe in mouth. She murmured and squinted as she slowly passed a bunch of basil leaves over Bunny. Bunny lay under a pile of patchwork quilts, her damp, platinum hair splayed on the pillows. Her eyes were half-closed, lips parted as she breathed. The room glowed from the light of healing candles laid on nearly every surface. The shadows danced. Weirdette lit the last candle on the dresser and waved her match to put it out. She scurried from the room and glared at Fairer Than.

"I'm fine," Bunny said. Her voice still rasped.

Fairer Than hung her head.

"Fairer Than," she heard Bunny say. When she looked at her, Bunny held out her hand, pale above the colorful patchworks.

"Just come," Bunny ordered.

Fairer Than did so. She looked away as she took Bunny's hand. She felt Bunny's cool, yet firm grasp, and Fairer Than experienced a lifting from her body. One of relief; joy. She was happy, angry, pained, and sad.

"You're warm," Bunny remarked. Her eyes closed.

Fairer Than watched Bunny breathe and fall asleep. She held Bunny's hand until Bunny was warm too.

An armored personnel carrier rumbled down one of the few paved roads cutting through the Enchanting Forest, its headlights lighting the road.

Dean sat in the front compartment, the windshield's metal shutters raised. Shang Yu bounced around in the front seat like a little boy. The carrier was one of a hodge-podge of military style vehicles lent to the Yu clan to take on the Huns. The swift responses from the other vampire houses had put an unsettled feeling in Dean's still stom-ach. It was happening so fast.

Just today, I thought I'd be in auto shop.

A part of her wanted to be excited when she saw the armored carrier, sitting out on the grass of the Steppes. Instead, she could only think of what Bunny would say if she saw it.

"What you think of your hot rods now, eh Yu Ying?" Shang Yu yelled from the front seat. Dean didn't answer and hunched in her leather jacket. She looked back at the drab, utilitarian interior, with its hard seats, weapons lock-ers, and hanging straps. Pop wanted to park the monster in the back of their *siheyuan* out of pure conceit, but she didn't doubt he had a bigger motive: getting Little Salem used to the sight of what was coming.

The carrier lurched, possibly from its wheels and weight digging another pothole into the road.

The towns aren't ready for this. This road—it's for travelers, hikers, Twilight World tourists.

It was for bike gangs, blissfully touring, looking for idle trouble. But the cold, hard vehicle she was riding in wasn't about brawls with werewolves. It wasn't about picking a fight with a dark faerie for hitting on her girl.

Another lurch rattled. Shang Yu giggled more and chattered in Chinese.

Who would end up filling the carrier's interior? Her friends Cesar, Danny—little Burt, the invisible boy? Out on the windy Steppes, Dean had dutifully followed Shang Yu and walked up and down before their motley Horde that stood at attention. Nearby, the Von Blaud's hussars and their horses practiced charging maneuvers. The number of fighters didn't seem enough for how many Huns were coming. The map in their home had become reality; it was all really happening.

She'd always known Pop to plot. Every evil creature in the Twilight World did, but they seemed to cause minor upheavals in minor kingdoms, like having to do with evil sorceress queens whose time had come. The Living Dead Huns was not like dealing with one evil queen.

Had the Twilight World ever had a real war? Dean wondered if she'd missed that detail in history class, but she had a sinking feeling there was no precedent. The Twilight World was what it was because there was a balance in effect. She'd watched a social studies film on it once, with cartoon characters that explained how it worked: strife was okay in the Twilight World as long as it came and went. The World always had to return to normal again. That was how their World endured, having come into being by powerful Words, spoken an unknown time ago.

Return to normal again. We can do that, she resolved.

When she looked out the windshield, the *Welcome to Little Salem* sign greeted her.

Bunny woke to a sore throat and a chest that hurt, but the smell of steeped eucalyptus filled the air, as well as the scent of healing candles. Did she sleep long?

Her cuckoo clock ticked. It was only nightfall. She turned her head to see if Aunt Hauntie still sat beside her and saw Fairer Than instead.

Fairer Than was still dressed in a sheet, her elbows on her knees and her hands clasped. Her green eyes were far away, as if she were ruminating. She sat on the small, wooden chair as easily as one would perch on a great throne. Her gaze slowly moved to meet Bunny's.

Before Bunny could speak, Fairer Than lifted something from the floor and placed it on Bunny's front. Bunny looked down. A sturdy wooden chest with hanging chains sat on her bosom. It was sealed with black wax and studded with thick nail heads.

"My heart," Fairer Than quietly said.

Bunny touched the chest in wonder. She attempted to sit up and Fairer Than reached to help her. Bunny then cradled the chest in both hands.

"My heart sits within a goose egg, inside this chest,

which once lay beneath a great stone, inside the man-eating maelstrom," Fairer Than explained. Her gaze fell. "I do not deserve it."

Bunny glanced at her, surprised, then looked at the chest again. The chest itself seemed as formidable as its owner. But when Fairer Than touched the lock, it dropped open with a simple click. She then broke the thick, wax seal by lifting the creaking lid, and Bunny saw the bright, white shell of the egg within, nestled in wool batting.

It looked fragile.

"It's beautiful," Bunny softly said.

"Keep it for me," Fairer Than said.

"Are you sure?" Bunny said, looking up.

"Yes."

Bunny nodded, feeling there was no reason to refuse, though the gravity of such responsibility gave her butterflies. Fairer Than rose, the conversation apparently ended.

"Fairer Than," Bunny said.

Fairer Than stopped.

"I'm sorry you're no longer a faerie," she said.

"That nature can be replaced with new things," Fairer Than said.

Bunny warmed, heartened. Fairer Than's gaze was still reluctant to meet hers.

Bunny gestured with the chest.

"This really contains your heart? And not a baby dragon?" Bunny gently asked.

"It is not a baby dragon," Fairer Than answered, nearly smiling.

"I shall keep it safe," Bunny promised.

♦

After Fairer Than departed, Bunny hid the chest behind her pillows. She was drinking the slippery elm tea that Aunt Agoosta had left her when someone mounted the creaking staircase, sucking noisily on a straw.

Sluuuurp, came the sound.

Honey walked into the bedroom, a Shivers milkshake in hand. When she saw Bunny, she stopped, laid the shake on the dresser, and came to sit on Bunny's bed. She had a spot of ketchup on the front of her blouse.

"Hi," Honey said, eyes downcast.

"I'm fine," Bunny said.

"If my getting lost ever puts Sugar in danger too, I'll go live on a deserted island," Honey declared. "This is too much when it involves family."

"I still don't know what's involved, and why it involves me," Bunny said gently.

Honey looked at her hands.

"I summoned Sugar to come pick me up. Usually I don't. Usually, I trust the Goddess to guide my way home. But this time, things are too complicated. This thing that I've seen foretold, it's bigger than all of us. If I get lost again, maybe I'll only help these events along more," Honey said fretfully.

"Honey," Bunny urged. "What did you come to tell me?"

Honey clasped Bunny's hand.

"Something terrible is coming," she said.

Bunny stared at her, searching her eyes.

"It hasn't happened already?" she gently asked

"Oh. Oh! Your near-drowning? Oh no, Bunny."

"What was foretold?" Bunny pressed.

"Death," Honey said. "Loss. Everywhere. What made us

content, safe here in the Twilight World, will be upset, the balance gone. I wish the answer to preventing these events were simple, as simple as getting rid of one evil, sorceress queen. But this time there's too much, and it will pull all of us in."

"Honey...why are you telling me this?"

Honey released Bunny's hand. She retrieved her pocket diary from her belt, the retractable chain whirring.

Honey opened the book and turned the pages.

"I'm telling you this," Honey said solemnly, "because when the time comes, you must fight the vampires."

She began to read.

♦

Fairer Than, dressed once more in her kirtle and bodice and with the Bakers' toolbox in hand, tested the newly repaired front door. It swung and shut properly, though she intended to make more permanent repair to the doorframe later. She touched the horseshoe nailed above.

Nothing. She moved down the moonlit garden for the broken front gate.

No bluebells tinkled at her presence. While preparing the gate's hinges for nailing back into its post, she listened for the sounds of insects singing, moonbeams cascading through the trees, and for the soft stirs that meant plant life was breathing.

She listened harder. No moonbeams or plants spoke.

When she looked towards the forest, her once-kin shimmered like fireflies between the trees.

The glamoured faeries traveled on, their laughter faint to her ears. Had she her faerie nature, she would see and hear them as clearly as if they stood before her. They did not bother to look her way, much less acknowledge her presence. She was a being outside their realm, right then.

If it puts Titania's fears of Bunny to rest, than what must be will be. She let her hammer express the finality of that decision, each blow sending a nail deep into the gate's post.

The cottage door creaked open and light spilled. Honey stepped out.

"Mission completed," she sighed. She approached.

"You are a most enigmatic herald." Fairer Than rose. She dropped her hammer into the toolbox and moved the gate to and fro.

"Sorry. I never had time to explain my mission to you. But then you've been switching bodies."

"Yes, I have been," Fairer Than said with a raised brow. "Because I felt the need to gallivant."

Honey raised her brow in turn.

"It's never apparent why I do something, but when I do, it serves its purpose," Honey said. "I came to Little Salem because evil's been foretold. You must have learned something about it when I cast the switch on you."

"I did." Fairer Than picked up the oil can. She oiled the hinges. "The vampires are up to no good, and Bunny loves one of them."

"They're going to start a war," Honey said.

Fairer Than looked away, recalling when she'd fought the Vikings, then the Normans, and finally had ridden out as a man on the first Crusade, a creature larking about with Christians, her last dalliance with war.

Never again, she'd promised at Brienne's grave.

"They are vampires," she said. "They do so not for glory,

nor for the purpose they will no doubt give to Little Salem: defense from those who would destroy us. They want to drain the town."

"It won't only be this town!" Honey exclaimed. "It will spread, because this is more than just sucking on money, or life, or happiness! It will affect the balance of the Twilight World. And if our world collapses, where will we go? You have to help stop this."

Fairer Than snorted.

"Had you asked me days ago, I would have been ambivalent. Matters like these that are motivated by evil, they rise, harm, destroy, and then ebb. Flowers grow again, and the sun returns. These things are of little concern to faerie. But thanks to you, I am no longer of the faerie," she added gruffly.

"Oh?" Honey stared, thoughts apparently running through her head. Then her expression softened. "I thought you seemed different."

"At the tavern, you thought it better had I killed Bunny's vampire." Fairer Than ignored Honey's look of sympathy. "Is that what you wish?"

Honey bit her lip. "That wasn't nice of me to say, was it? And no, don't you dare make me your reason. Look, I don't know if—well, if Dean were to run away *right now*, would that change things? This is big. Oh so big. Don't big things happen because of several things? Maybe Dean is just one thing, and her moment to change all this is past."

"Perhaps, but a *ruler* can make the change you wish. One need only vanquish those who disagree, then extinguish the problem." Fairer Than walked back to the Baker's front door to set the toolbox beside it. Honey followed.

"Easier said by a dragon-being. But *your* not being a faerie anymore…" The grave look on Honey's face was much like Bunny's. "What does that mean?"

Yes, what does it mean? Fairer Than had given Bunny her heart.

"I would do anything for her," she said, looking into the night.

Honey sighed. "I guess that's good. I just do what I do. Honey the Flukey. But this time, with your losing your faerie nature and Bunny nearly drowning…I'm not sure if I'm meant to do right."

Fairer Than looked at her skeptically.

"You are the one who evil least expects, poking holes in the darkness so that light may shine through," she said. "We know more, thanks to you. Never doubt your power, Honey Baker."

Honey smiled.

"You're not so bad for a dragon-thing."

Rubber wheels approached. A small battered car pulled up in the far distance, its headlights wavering.

"Sugar's here!" Honey exclaimed. "That's my sister. She's taking me home, but first she needs to see Bunny."

Honey hurried through the repaired garden gate, waving to the car's occupant. Fairer Than watched her go, reluctant to meet this third Baker woman. Too many witches were not healthy for an ex-faerie. Her former mix of breeding had once made her, she belatedly realized, quite inviolate. She was halved with her faerie powers gone.

She headed in another direction and hopped the stonewall. Yet her departure from the Baker cottage felt different, and perhaps it had nothing to do with Bunny's aunties forgetting to chase her and soak her. Her chest's ghost-ache had lessened. Bunny had accepted her heart's egg. But what comforted most, no thanks to herself, was the fact that Bunny was alive, and Fairer Than kept that thought a precious treasure in the cavity of her once-heart.

Her fire had returned, the black embers within relit with new purpose. She quickly returned to the lake with a dragon's gaze that spied slumbering creatures as pulsing orange balls in their warm burrows. An owl took flight above, a hot yellow streak moving powerfully across the night sky. She would talk to Lady. Then she would abandon her forest bower. Goodie Gertie, whom she sometimes did handy work for, had a barn she could retire in.

Come morning, she'd find the two faerie men and deliver unto them a most entertaining retribution.

After Honey left, Bunny retrieved her princess phone and placed it in her lap.

She picked up the receiver, hesitated, put it back in its cradle, and then picked up the receiver again. She dialed Dean's number.

She listened to the rings and the pounding of her heart.

The phone clicked as someone picked up.

"Hey," Dean answered eagerly.

"I wanted to check on you sooner," Bunny said, relieved. "But things happened after you were pushed back into your own body." She hesitated, wondering how to share something like nearly drowning. Somehow, she was not upset, despite how awful the experience had been. After hearing Honey's message, her near-death was a small matter right then.

"Yeah, I'm back in my own body now." Dean's tone seemed weary. "And I'm sorry I couldn't get away. Pop abducted me again and took me to inspect our Horde. I just got back. But now everything's okay, right? Spell all gone?"

"It is," Bunny said. "Completed and closed. But you're okay?" She wondered why Dean sounded sad.

Once Dean assured her all was well, Bunny explained what happened at the lake.

Dean was understandably upset, and after many assurances that Bunny was all right, that Fairer Than was not to blame but had saved her life, and that Dean needn't come right then (especially with Honey and Fairer Than present) Dean finally calmed down. Bunny heard the distinct rattle of Sugar's old car and knew it was time to bring up what was foremost in her mind.

"Dean?"

"Yeah?"

"I've heard something," Bunny said. "Something about the vampires that might be serious."

"Oh…? Fairer Than learned something when she was in my body, didn't she?"

"Never mind that. What's going on?"

"Well. There's this—a vampire thing. Kinda serious, but well, stuff always looks like that between these old guys, and then you realize everyone's bluffing. To get what they want, y'know?"

"'Serious'?" Bunny repeated. *Tell me, Dean.*

"I can't say more. But I don't think anything will happen, Bunny."

"What makes you think that, Dean?"

"Because I'm not going to let it happen. Gotta keep the

world safe for you."

Bunny smiled. "Who knew you were my superhero?"

"I'm learnin'." She heard the grin in Dean's voice. "Do you know why I love you?"

Bunny settled into her bed. "Tell me again."

"Because you're everything I'm missing. You're warmth and sunshine and birds singing, and pies—you're breath and life. I get all that when I'm with you."

Bunny couldn't speak. She thought Dean's voice cracked a little.

"I gotta go," Dean said cheerfully. "See you at school, tomorrow?"

"Yes," Bunny said softly.

"Love you."

"Love you too."

Dean hung up, and Bunny slowly put down the receiver.

Dean stared at her black phone, her hand still on the receiver.

Bunny. Nearly drowned.

She'd run over to the Baker cottage tonight, despite Bunny's protests. Peek in while Bunny lay asleep. Make sure she was okay.

With Bunny sleeping, Dean wouldn't have to further discuss that "something" Fairer Than had learned about. How to share that the world had suddenly gone upside down, and she wasn't sure if she could get it right side up again?

Dean sat on her coffin bed with her hand still on the receiver.

She forced her body to take a deep breath, inhaling and remembering the fire in Fairer Than's chest. When she exhaled, her body felt as still and silent as before.

She missed the singing sunlight, the gift of breath, of beating heart and blood and...her vanquished blood-thirst, most of all.

She sat with her hand on the receiver, her new straight sword gleaming on the chair before her. On the floor lay her new armor.

"This is what we're fighting for," she said.

♦

"Inky," Bunny said warmly as her black cat suddenly hopped atop the quilts and took the place of the princess phone. Inky purred as Bunny stroked her back.

"If you had died, I would have taken good care of your clothes," Inky said. Bunny hugged her. Someone mounted the steps with the light click of female high heels.

Inky jumped off Bunny's lap. Bunny held out her arms for Sugar as her eldest cousin entered the room. Sugar, so very smart and professor-like, smelled of golden, woody amber and flowery vanilla. Black cat eye frames, red lip-stick, silk stockings, and herringbone skirt and jacket—unlike Bunny and Honey, Sugar was tall, athletic of build, and simply *important* looking. The rest of the Baker cous-ins (like Venetian blonde Sunny and golden-haired Dew) were light haired. Sugar's hair was dark; her brunette locks worn in a chignon. Bunny hated the stereotype about blondes and their brains, yet Dr. Baker was the smartest of them all, both in academics and the secrets of the uni-verse. She had time-traveled. She had gone not just beyond their Twilight World but also beyond their planet. Sugar had reputedly saved galaxies. Bunny couldn't help hugging Sugar a little longer, wishing her cousin would take care of everything.

"Darlin', how're you doing?" Sugar asked warmly.

Though she assured her cousin she was all right, Sugar moved her hands to trace Bunny's body. When she pulled both hands away, fingers snapping, Bunny felt snapped into place. Stale breath left her that she didn't know she still harbored, tasting like the last of the maelstrom's water. Bunny lightened.

Honey, Sugar, and their aunties then brought chairs in and sat around Bunny's bed. Sugar drew a great sphere in the air above Bunny's head. Her drawing fingers formed one great circle, then another intersecting the first, and finally the stabilizing circumference within. She touched Bunny's forehead.

"Now think on it, darlin'," she said.

Bunny did, her memories replaying in the sphere. She showed them how she'd fled the faerie hollow, met Fairer Than at the lake, their conversation in the boat, and then her accident. Sharing all of her argument with Fairer Than was hard enough, but the drowning was even harder. When the sphere went dark, Sugar prompted her to recall more. Bunny did, remembering her painful awakening and how she saw the shining relief in Fairer Than's eyes.

How I saw love.

She ended the recollection abruptly. The replay blanked from the air above. Sugar and Honey smiled. But Aunt Weirdette clucked and Aunt Agoosta sighed.

"What's this about the vampires, then?" Hauntette said

darkly.

Honey opened her pocket diary. When she spoke, Aunt Weirdie clucked more and Hauntette smoked, her pipe a puffing chimney. Inky settled in Sugar's lap and purred.

Bunny picked up the orange, bag of cloves, and a long red ribbon she'd retrieved earlier from her sewing basket and had placed on her nightstand. She wrapped and tied the orange, then pushed cloves into the orange's skin in neat lines while listening. Each time she pricked the orange she thought of Dean, but Fairer Than's words of being a bleeding pincushion came to mind.

No, she thought reassuringly to the once-faerie. She pushed more cloves in and thought of them both.

When she'd finished studding the orange in patterns, Sugar spoke.

"Bunny must help Dean stop the vampires," she said.

The aunties said nothing, though Aunt Hauntie chewed unhappily on her pipe stem.

"Well, I thought—never mind," Honey said.

Bunny reached up. She hung the pomander from her bedpost. The scent of orange and cloves filled the air.

"I know Sugar's being diplomatic," Bunny said. "And I know what you're all thinking."

She thought of Dean, and then of their world.

"I'll do it," she said. "I'll fight every vampire."

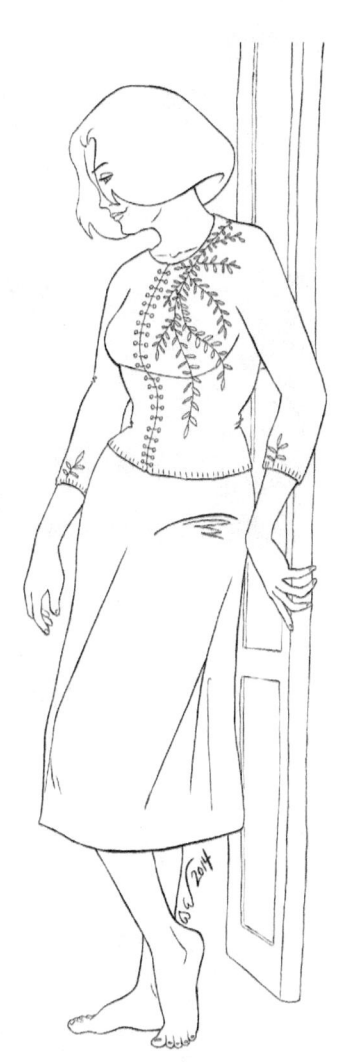

Read more in
Charm School Graphique Vol 1
and
Charm School Digital No 1-9

More from Elizabeth:
The Wrecking Faerie: A Charm School Novella Vol 1
Hot Roddin' To Hell: A Charm School Novella Vol 2

The Dark Victorian: Risen Vol 1
The Dark Victorian: Bones Vol 2
Ice Demon: A Dark Victorian Penny Dread Vol 1
Medusa: A Dark Victorian Penny Dread Vol 2
Sundark: An Elle Black Penny Dread Vol 1
Poison Garden: An Elle Black Penny Dread Vol 2
Monster Stalker: A Darquepunk Novel Vol 1
Fae Came On the Plane! A Darquepunk Novella

Author's Notes

Charm School, the comic book:

Charm School the comic book was originally published by Slave Labor Graphics (SLG Publishing) from 1999 to 2003. Written and drawn by me, there were nine issues, with a tenth and final issue long promised. Bunny first appeared in the comic book short story, *Bunny the Good Li'l Teen Witch*, published in *Action Girl Comics* #13 in 1997, also by SLG Publishing.

This novelization of the third *Charm School* story arc, *Body Chase: The Fall of Fairer Than*, goes beyond the comic book issues which end at #9. #10 was never published and as I write this, remains in thumbnail rough form, still ready for final pencils and inking. For many Charm School readers, that marks about fifteen years of waiting for the conclusion.

About The Author

Elizabeth Watasin is the author of the Gothic steampunk series *The Dark Victorian*, The *Elle Black Penny Dreads*, the *Darquepunk* series, and the creator/artist of the indie comics series *Charm School*. She is the winner of the 2015 Rainbow Award for Best Lesbian Fantasy and Romance Fantasy and a Gaylactic Spectrum nominee. A twenty year veteran of animation and comics, her credits include thirteen feature films, such as *Beauty and the Beast*, *Aladdin*, *The Lion King*, and *The Princess and the Frog*, and writing for *Disney Adventures* magazine. She lives in Los Angeles with her black cat named Draw, bringing readers uncanny heroines in cyberpunk, historical fantasy, diesal fantasy, and paranormal thrillers.

Sign up for the mailing list at A-Girl Studio.
www.a-girlstudio.com
amazon.com/author/elizabethwatasin
www.facebook.com/ElizabethWatasinX
twitter.com/ewatasin

Paperback versions contain
illustration galleries.

ELIZABETH WATASIN

The DARK VICTORIAN
SERIES

Amazon
Barnes & Noble
iBookstore

Learn more at
A-girlstudio.com.

Bringing you uncanny heroines in shilling shocker mysteries,
paranormal romance, and Steampunk adventuress tales.

ELIZABETH WATASIN

The DARK VICTORIAN

BONES

www.ingramcontent.com/pod-product-compliance
Lightning Source LLC
Chambersburg PA
CBHW020406130626
46549CB00006B/2454